A BABY TO HEAL
THEIR HEARTS

BY
KATE HARDY

MILLS
BOON®

First published in Great Britain 2015
by Mills & Boon, an imprint of Harlequin (UK) Limited,
Large Print edition 2015
Eton House, 18-24 Paradise Road
Richmond, Surrey, TW9 1SR

© 2015 Pamela Brooks

ISBN: 978-0-263-25496-9

Harlequin (UK) Limited's policy is to use papers that are natural, renewable and recyclable products and made from wood grown in sustainable forests. The logging and manufacturing processes conform to the legal environmental regulations of the country of origin.

Printed and bound in Great Britain
by CPI Antony Rowe, Chippenham, Wiltshire

'Bailey, I really want to kiss you,' he whispered.

'I want you to kiss me, too,' she whispered back.

That was all the encouragement he needed. He dipped his head again, and took his sweet time kissing her. Every brush of his mouth against hers, every nibble, made him more and more aware of her. And she was kissing him back, her arms wrapped as tightly round him as his were round her.

He wanted this to last for ever.

But then he became aware that the music had changed and become more up-tempo, and he and Bailey were still swaying together as if the band was playing a slow dance. He broke the kiss, and he could see the exact moment that she realised what was going on, too. Those gorgeous dark eyes were absolutely huge. And she looked as shocked as he felt. Panicked, almost.

This wasn't supposed to be happening.

'I…um…' she said, and tailed off.

'Yeah.' He didn't know what to say either. What he really wanted to do was kiss her again…

Dear Reader

When I wrote IT STARTED WITH NO STRINGS... I was drawn to the heroine's best friend, Bailey Randall—she's one of these irrepressibly cheerful people (quite like me!) and, given that she loves the gym and dance-based classes (ahem...again, quite like me!), I really had to give in and write her story.

But Bailey's irrepressible cheeriness hides a deep sadness. And when she meets seemingly dour Scot Jared Fraser she discovers that he's hiding a few things, too. She doesn't think she can give him what he wants out of life, he completely misreads her, and yet they discover that they can't resist each other. When Bailey's worst nightmare and Jared's deepest dream come true, will they realise that they could end up healing each other's hearts?

I hope you enjoy their story.

I'm always delighted to hear from readers, so do come and visit me at www.katehardy.com

With love

Kate Hardy

Kate Hardy lives in Norwich, in the east of England, with her husband, two young children, one bouncy spaniel and too many books to count! When she's not busy writing romance or researching local history she helps out at her children's schools. She also loves cooking—spot the recipes sneaked into her books! (They're also on her website, along with extracts and stories behind the books.)

Writing for Mills & Boon® has been a dream come true for Kate—something she wanted to do ever since she was twelve. She's been writing Medical Romances™ for over ten years now. She says it's the best of both worlds, because she gets to learn lots of new things when she's researching the background to a book: add a touch of passion, drama and danger, a new gorgeous hero every time, and it's the perfect job!

Kate's always delighted to hear from readers, so do drop in to her website at www.katehardy.com

Recent titles by Kate Hardy:

Mills & Boon® Medical Romance™

IT STARTED WITH NO STRINGS…
200 HARLEY STREET: THE SOLDIER PRINCE
HER REAL FAMILY CHRISTMAS
A DATE WITH THE ICE PRINCESS
THE BROODING DOC'S REDEMPTION
ONCE A PLAYBOY…
DR CINDERELLA'S MIDNIGHT FLING

Mills & Boon® Cherish™

BEHIND THE FILM STAR'S SMILE
BOUND BY A BABY
BALLROOM TO BRIDE AND GROOM

These books are also available in eBook format from www.millsandboon.co.uk

To C.C. Coburn and Cathleen Ross—
hope you enjoy Herod!

**Praise for
Kate Hardy:**

'BOUND BY A BABY moved me to
tears many times. It is a full-on emotional
drama. Author Kate Hardy brought this
tale shimmering with emotions. Highly
recommended for all lovers of romance.'
—*Contemporary Romance Reviews*

**BOUND BY A BABY
won the 2014 RoNA
(Romantic Novelists' Association) Rose award!**

'When you pick up a romance novel
by Kate Hardy you know that you're
going to be reading a spellbinding novel
which you will want to devour in a
single sitting and A CHRISTMAS KNIGHT
is certainly no exception.'
—*CataRomance*

CHAPTER ONE

'SHE'S A BONNY LASS, our Bailey,' Archie said.

Jared's heart sank at the expression on the coach's face. Clearly Archie had taken a fancy to the researcher. And Jared had a nasty feeling that this might be a case of the coach's libido taking over from his common sense.

Allegedly, this 'bonny lass' researcher had a system that could reduce soft-tissue injuries among the players. So far, so good—but the figures being bandied about were crazy. In Jared's experience, when something sounded too good to be true, it usually was. And he could really do without some pretty, flaky girl distracting the players and getting in the way when he needed to treat them. Especially when he'd only just started his new job as the doctor to the youth team of a premiership division football club.

He'd been here before, when a manager's or player's head had been turned by a pretty girl, and the outcome was always messy. Worse still, it tended to have an impact on the rest of the team. With a bunch of teenage lads, this could get very messy indeed.

But he kept his thoughts to himself and gave the coach a polite smile. 'That's nice.'

Hopefully this Bailey woman would get bored quickly, or her system would be debunked, and they could go back to a more sensible way of preventing soft-tissue injuries—like sport-specific training, after he'd assessed each of the players and taken a proper medical history.

In the meantime, he'd have to grit his teeth and be as polite and as neutral as possible.

'Bailey—oh, good, you're here. Come and meet Jared Fraser, the new team doctor,' Archie McLennan called over from the side of the football pitch as Bailey walked through the players' tunnel.

Bailey smiled at the youth team's coach, but

she made sure that she stood just far enough away so that Archie couldn't put his arm round her shoulders. She liked him very much as a colleague—he was at least prepared to listen to new ideas and he'd been more than fair with her on the research project so far—but she really wasn't in the market for a relationship.

Particularly with someone who was recently divorced and with a lifestyle that really didn't work for her; that was just setting things up to fail. And Bailey had failed quite enough in her relationships, thank you very much. She wanted life to be simple in the future—full of her family, her friends and her work, and that was enough for her. She didn't need anything more.

'Jared, this is Bailey Randall—the doctor whose research project I was telling you about,' Archie said.

For a moment, Jared looked as if he'd seen a ghost. Then he seemed to pull himself together and gave her a brief nod of acknowledgement. 'Dr Randall.'

But he didn't smile at her. Did he not approve of women being involved with a football team? Was he not good at social skills? Or—given that his accent was quite distinctive—was he just living up to the stereotype of the slightly dour, strong-and-silent Scotsman?

It was a shame, because he had the most gorgeous eyes. A deep, intense blue—the colour of a bluebell carpet. If he smiled, she'd just bet his eyes would have an irresistible twinkle.

Which was crazy. Since when did she think so fancifully? Bluebells, indeed.

'Pleased to meet you,' she said, giving him her brightest smile, and held her hand out for him to shake.

He gave another brief inclination of his head and shook her hand. His grip was firm, brief and very businesslike. He still didn't smile, though. Or say any kind of social pleasantry.

Oh, well. It wasn't as if she'd need to have that much to do with him, was it? Her project—to test a monitoring system to see if it could help to reduce the number of soft-tissue injuries in the team—had been agreed by the football club's chair of directors. She'd been working with Archie, the youth team coach, at training sessions and on match days when they played at home, and so far the system's results were proving very interesting indeed.

'Hey, Bailey.' John, one of the players, came over to the side and high-fived her.

'Hey, John. How's the ankle?' she asked.

'It's holding up, thanks to you,' he said with a smile.

'And you're still wearing that support?'

He nodded. 'And I'm doing the wobble-board exercises, like you showed me last time,' he said.

'Good.'

'Bailey helped out on a couple of sessions when she was here and your predecessor called in sick,' Archie told Jared. 'John sprained his ankle a few weeks back.'

'Sprained ankles are the most common injury in football,' Bailey said, just so Jared Fraser would know that she did actually understand the situation—maybe he was the dinosaur kind of man who thought that women knew next to nothing about sport. 'He was running when he hit a bump in the field, the sole of his foot rolled under and the movement damaged the ligaments on the outside of his ankle.' She shrugged. 'The wobble-board training we've been doing reduces the risk of him damaging his ankle again.'

Jared gave her another of those brief nods, but otherwise he was completely impassive.

Oh, great. How on earth was he going to connect with the players? Or maybe he was better at communicating when he was in work mode, being a doctor. She certainly hoped so, because the boys were still young enough to need encouragement and support; they weren't likely to respond to dourness.

'I ought to give you each other's mobile phone numbers and email addresses and what have you—in case you need to discuss anything,' Archie said.

'I doubt we will,' Jared said, 'but fine.'

Oh, what was *the guy's problem?* She itched to shake him, but that wouldn't be professional. Particularly in front of the youth team. Doctors, coaches and managers were supposed to present a united front. OK, so strictly speaking she didn't work for the football club—she was here purely as a researcher—but she still needed to be professional. 'Give me your number,' she said, 'and I'll text you with my email address so you have all my details.'

Once that was sorted out, she took her laptop out of its case. 'OK, guys, you know the drill. Let's go.' As the players lined up, she switched on her laptop, then called each team member by name and handed him a monitor with a chest strap, checking each one in with the laptop as she went.

'So what exactly is this system?' Jared asked when the players had filed onto the field to warm up. 'Some kind of glorified pedometer, like those expensive wristband gadgets that tell people they woke up three times during the night, but don't actually tell them why they woke up or what they can do about it?'

He sounded downright hostile. *What was his problem?* she thought again. But she gritted her teeth and tried her best to be polite. 'It does measure the number of steps the players take, yes,' she said, 'but it also monitors their average speed, the average steps they take per game, their heart rate average and maximum, and their VO2.' VO2 measured the amount of oxygen used by the body to convert the energy from food into adenosine triphosphate; the higher the VO2 max, the higher the athlete's level of fitness.

He scoffed. 'How on earth can you measure VO2 properly without hooking someone up to a system with a mask?'

'It's an estimate,' she admitted, 'but this system is a lot more than just a "glorified pedometer".' She put exaggerated quotes round the phrase with her fingers, just to make the point that she wasn't impressed by his assessment. Sure, once he knew what the system did and how it worked, she'd be happy to listen to him and to any suggestions he might have for improving it. But right now he was speaking from a position of being totally uninformed, so how could his opinion be in the least bit valid?

'The point is,' she said, 'to look at reducing the number of soft-tissue injuries. That means the players get more time to train and play, and they spend less time recovering from injuries. This particular system has been tested with a rugby team and it reduced their soft-tissue injury rate by seventy per cent, and my boss thinks it's worth giving it a try on other sports.' She gave him a grim smile. 'Just so you know, I'm not trying to put you out of a job. If anything, I'm trying to make your life easier by taking out the small, time-consuming stuff.'

'And you're actually a qualified doctor?' he asked, sounding sceptical.

Give me strength, Bailey thought, but she gave him another polite smile. 'Remind me to bring my degree certificate in with me next time,' she said. 'Or you can look me up on the Internet, if you're that fussed. I run sports medicine clinics three days a week at the London Victoria, so you'll find me listed in the department there, and I spend the other two working days each week on a research project.'

'So you're using this system of yours with other teams as well?' he asked.

'No—this is the only team I'm working with, and I only do one research project at a time. My last one was preventative medicine,' she explained. 'Basically I worked with patients who had high blood pressure. The aim was to help them to lose weight and maintain lean muscle mass, and that reduced both their blood pressure and their risk of cardiovascular incidents.' She couldn't resist adding, 'And by that I mean heart attacks and strokes.'

'Right.' Jared stared at Bailey. Archie had called her a 'bonny lass', but she was so much more than that. She was truly beautiful, with a heart-shaped face and huge brown eyes—emphasised by her elfin crop. She looked more like some glamorous Mediterranean princess than a doctor.

But, in Jared's experience, beautiful women spelled trouble and heartache. His ex, Sasha, had used her stunning looks to get her own way—and Jared had fallen for it hard enough to get very badly burned. Nowadays he was pretty much impervious to huge eyes and winsome smiles. But he'd already seen how Archie was following Bailey round like a lapdog; he had a nasty feeling that Bailey Randall had used her looks to get her own way with her ridiculous bit of computerised kit, the way Sasha always used her looks.

Still, at least this system of hers wasn't something that would actually hurt the players. It wouldn't be of much real use—like the pricey fitness wristbands he'd referred to earlier, it wouldn't give enough information about what was actually wrong or how to fix it—but it wouldn't do any real harm, either.

Jared spent the session on the side of the pitch, ready in case any of the players had an injury that needed treating. But there were no strains, sprains or anything more serious; and, at the other end of the scale, there wasn't even a bruise or a contusion.

Half a lifetime ago, he'd been one of them, he thought wryly. A young hopeful, planning a career in the sport and dreaming of playing for his country. He'd actually made it and played for the England under-nineteen squad, scoring several goals in international matches. But Bailey Randall's bit of kit wouldn't have done anything to save him from the knee injury in his final game—the tackle that had stopped his football career in its tracks. Jared had ended up pursuing his original plans instead, studying for his A-levels and following in the family tradition by taking a degree in medicine.

The lure of football had drawn Jared to work with a club as their team doctor, rather than working in a hospital or his parents' general practice. And he still enjoyed the highs and lows of the game, the camaraderie among the players and hearing the supporters roar their approval when a goal was scored.

At the end of the training session, Archie turned to Bailey. 'Over to you.'

Jared watched in sheer disbelief as Bailey proceeded to take the youth team through a series of yoga stretches and then breathing exercises.

What place did yoga have on a football pitch? In his experience, the players would do far better working on sport-specific training. As well as ball control, they needed to focus on muscular endurance and lower-body strength, and also work on explosive acceleration and short bursts of speed. If Archie wanted him to do it, Jared could design a training programme easily enough—either a warm-up routine that would work for the whole team, or some player-specific programmes to help deal with each player's weak spots—and it would do a lot more for the players' overall neuromuscular co-ordination than yoga would.

But having a go at Bailey Randall in front of the team wouldn't be professional, so Jared kept his mouth shut until the lads had gone for a shower and she was doing things on her laptop. Then he walked over to her and said, 'Can we have a quick word?'

She looked up from her laptop with an expression of surprise, but nodded. 'Sure.'

'What *exactly* does your box of tricks tell us?' he asked.

'It analyses each player's performance. For each player, I can show you a graph of his average performance over the last ten matches or training sessions, and how today's performance compares against that average.'

So far, so good. 'Which tells us what?'

'The system will pick up if a player is underperforming,' she said. 'Maybe he's coming down with a cold but isn't showing any symptoms yet—and if he's sick he's more at risk of sustaining injury and shouldn't be playing.'

He gave her a sceptical look. 'So you're telling me you can predict if a player's going to get a cough or a cold?'

'No, but I can predict the likelihood of the

player sustaining an injury in his next match, based on his performance today and measured against an average of his last ten sessions.'

'Right.' Jared still wasn't totally convinced. And then he tackled the subject that bothered him most about today's antics. 'And the yoga?'

'As a football team doctor—someone who's clearly specialised in sports medicine—you'd already know that dynamic stretches are more useful than static stretches.' She held his gaze. 'But if you want me to spell it out to prove that I know what I'm talking about, dynamic stretches means continuous movement. That promotes blood flow, strength and stability. It also means you can work on more than one muscle group at a time—so it's more functional, because it mimics what happens with everyday movements. And you only hold the stretch for a short period of time, so the muscle releases more effectively and you get a better range of movement with each repetition.' She raised her eyebrows, as if challenging him to call her on it. 'Happy?'

He nodded. She did at least know her stuff, then. Even if she was a bit misguided about the computer programme. 'So you're a qualified yoga teacher?'

'No. But a qualified teacher—the one who's taught me for the last five years—helped me put the routine together.'

'Right. And the breathing?'

She put her hands on her hips and gave him a hard stare. 'Oh, for goodness' sake! Are you going to quiz me on every aspect of this? Look, the project's already been approved by Mr Fincham.' The chairman of the club's board of directors. 'If you have a problem with it, then maybe you need to speak to him about it.'

'I just don't see what use yoga is going to be to a bunch of lads who need sport-specific training,' he said.

'"Lads" being the operative word,' she said. 'They're sixteen, seventeen—technically they're not quite adults, and most of their peers are either still in education or starting some kind of apprenticeship. I won't insult them by calling them children, because they're not, but they still have quite a lot of growing up to do. And, in the profession they've chosen, they're all very much in the public eye. The media hounds are just waiting to tear into the behaviour of over-paid footballers, whipping up a frenzy among their readers about how badly the boys behave.'

'That's true,' he said, 'but I still don't get what it has to do with yoga.'

'Discipline,' she said crisply.

'They already have the discipline of turning up for training and doing what Archie tells them to do.'

'Holding the yoga poses also takes discipline, and so does the breathing. So it's good practice and it helps to underline what Archie does with them. Plus it's good for helping to deal with stress,' she said.

That was the bit Jared really didn't buy into.

She clearly saw the scepticism in his expression, because she sighed. 'Look, if they get hassled by photographers or journalists or even just someone else in a club when they're out—someone who wants to prove himself as a big hero who can challenge a footballer and beat him up—then all they have to do is remember to breathe and it'll help them to take everything down a notch.'

'Hmm,' he said, still not convinced.

She threw her hands up in apparent disgust. 'You know what? You can think what you like, Dr Fraser. It's not going to make any difference to my research. If you've got some good ideas for how the data can be used, or about different measurements that would be useful in analysing the team's performance, then I'd be very happy to listen. But if all you're going to do is moan and bitch, then please just go and find someone else to annoy, because I'm busy. Excuse me.'

Bailey Randall clearly didn't like it when someone actually questioned her. And she still hadn't convinced him of the benefits of her project. 'Of course you are,' he said, knowing how nasty it sounded but right at that moment not caring.

As he walked away, he was sure he heard her mutter, 'What an ass.'

She was entitled to her opinion. He wasn't very impressed by her, either. But they'd just have to make the best of it, for as long as it took for Archie and the team director to realise that her 'research' was all a load of hokum.

CHAPTER TWO

'HE'S IMPOSSIBLE. TALK about blinkered. And narrow-minded. And—and— Arrgh!' Bailey stabbed her fork into her cake in utter frustration.

To her dismay, Joni just laughed.

'You're my best friend,' Bailey reminded her. 'You're supposed to be supportive.'

'I am. Of course I am,' Joni soothed. 'But you're the queen of endorphins. You always see the best in people, and to see you having a hissy fit about someone—well, he's obviously made quite an impression on you.'

'And not a good one.' Bailey ate a forkful of cake and then rolled her eyes at the plate. 'Oh, come on. If I'm going to eat this stuff, it could at least reward me with a sugar rush.'

'Maybe it just makes you grumpy.'

Bailey narrowed her eyes at her best friend. 'Now you're laughing at me.'

Joni reached over the table and hugged her. 'I love you, and you're in an almighty strop. Which doesn't happen very often. This Jared Fraser guy has really rattled you.'

Bailey glowered. 'Honestly. He quizzed me on every single aspect of my project.'

'Which is better than just dismissing it.'

'He *did* dismiss it, actually. He thinks the players should be doing sport-specific training.'

Joni coughed. 'You're the sports medicine doctor, not me. And I seem to remember you saying something about sport-specific training being the most effective.'

'But it's not the only kind of training they should be doing,' Bailey said. 'Yoga means dynamic stretches, which are more effective than static ones. And there's the discipline of holding the pose and doing the breathing. It's really good for the boys, and it helps them to focus.'

'Maybe you should make Jared do the stuff

with the boys,' Joni suggested. 'And you can make him do extra planks.'

'Don't tempt me.' Bailey ate more cake. 'Actually, Joni, that might be a good idea. He needs to chill out a bit. Downward dog and breathing—that would do the trick.'

'I'd love to be a fly on the wall when you suggest it to him,' Joni said.

'No, you wouldn't. You hate people fighting—and he really doesn't like me.'

'You don't like him, either,' Joni pointed out.

'Well, no. Because he's rude, arrogant and narrow-minded. With men like him around, I'm more than happy to stay single.'

They both knew that wasn't the real reason why Bailey was resolutely single. After her life had imploded two and a half years ago, her marriage had cracked beyond repair. And Bailey still wasn't ready to risk trying another relationship. She didn't know if she ever would be.

'I don't know what to say,' Joni said, giving her another hug, 'except I love you and I believe in you.'

'You, too,' Bailey said.

'And I worry about you. That you're lonely.'

'That's because you're all loved up. Which is just as it should be,' Bailey said, 'given that it's just under two months until you get married to Aaron. And he's a sweetie.'

'Even so, I worry about you, Bailey.'

'I'm fine,' Bailey said, forcing herself to smile. 'Just grumpy tonight. And don't breathe a word of this to my mum, or she'll say that I'm attracted to Jared Fraser and I'm in denial about it.'

'Are you?' Joni asked.

Bailey blew out a breath. 'You're about the only person who could get away with asking that. No. He might be nice looking if he smiled,' she said, 'and to be fair he does have nice eyes. The colour of bluebells. But even if he was as sweet as Aaron, I still wouldn't be interested. I'm fine exactly as I am. I don't need anyone to complicate my life.'

Her words were slightly hollow, and she was pretty sure that Joni would pick up on that. But to her relief Joni didn't push it any further, or comment on that stupid remark she'd made about bluebells.

She wasn't attracted to Jared Fraser. She wanted to give him a good shake and tell him to open his mind a bit.

And bluebells were out of the question.

Before the next match, Bailey had a meeting with Archie to discuss the latest results from her software. As she'd half expected, Jared was there. Still playing dour, strong and silent. Well, that was his problem. She had a job to do.

'Travis is underperforming,' she said, showing them the graph on her laptop screen. 'It might be that he's had too many late nights over the last week, or it might be that he's coming down with something—but I'd recommend that he doesn't play as part of the team today.'

'I've already assessed the squad this morning, and they're all perfectly fit,' Jared said.

'A player who's underperforming is at a greater risk of soft-tissue injury,' she reminded him.

'According to your theory. Which has yet to be proven, because if you pull a player off every time they do a few steps less per game, then of course he won't get a soft-tissue injury, because he won't actually be playing. And if you follow that through every time, you'll end up with a really tiny pool of players. And the rest of them won't have had enough practice to help them improve their skills.'

'If they're off for weeks with an injury, that's not going to help them improve their skills, either,' she pointed out.

'Travis is fine.' He folded his arms. 'You're making a fuss over nothing.'

'Travis *isn't* fine.' She mirrored his defensive stance. 'But it isn't our call. It's Archie's.'

'Fine,' Jared said.

Archie looked at them both and sighed. 'I'll have a word with the lad.'

Clearly Travis was desperate to play, because Archie came back to tell them that the boy was in the team.

If Jared said 'Told you so', she might just punch him.

He didn't. But it was written all over his face.

Cross, Bailey sat on the bench at the side of the pitch and texted her best friend: Jared Fraser has to be the most smug, self-satisfied man in the universe.

A few seconds later, her phone beeped. She glanced at the screen, expecting Joni to have sent her a chin-up-and-rise-above-it type of message, and was surprised to see that the message was from Jared Fraser. Why would he be texting her? He was sitting less than six feet away from her. He could lean across and talk to her. He didn't need to resort to texting.

Curious, she opened the message. Herod?

What?

Don't understand, she texted back. Ridiculous man. What was he on about?

Her phone beeped a few seconds later. Your message: <<Herod Fraser has to be the most smug, self-satisfied man in the universe.>>

Then she realised exactly what had just happened.

Oh, no.

She'd been typing so fast that she obviously hadn't noticed her phone autocorrecting 'Jared' to 'Herod'. And Jared's name was right next to Joni's in her phone book. When Bailey had tapped on the recipient box, she'd clearly pressed the wrong name on the screen.

So now Jared Fraser knew exactly what she thought about him.

Which could make life very awkward indeed.

Sorry, she typed back. Not that she was apologising for what she'd said. She stood by every word of that—well, bar the autocorrected name. She was only apologising for her mistake.

Didn't mean to send that to you.

I'd already worked that one out for myself.

She sneaked a glance at him to see if she could work out how much he was going to make her pay for that little error, and was shocked to realise that he was actually smiling. He wasn't angry or even irritated; he was amused.

There was a sudden rush of feeling in her stomach, as if champagne was fizzing through her veins instead of blood. Totally ridiculous. But when the man smiled, it changed him totally. Rather than being the dour, hard-faced, slightly intimidating man she'd instinctively disliked, he was beautiful.

Oh, help. She really couldn't afford to let her thoughts go in that direction. For all she knew, he could be married or at least involved with someone. She knew nothing about the man, other than that he was the new youth team doctor and he didn't believe in her research at all.

'Sir, are you *the* Jared Fraser?' Billy, one of the substitutes, asked, coming over to sit in the pointedly large gap on the bench between Bailey and Jared.

The Jared Fraser? Why would there be something special about a football team's doctor? Bailey wondered.

'How do you mean?' Jared asked.

'Me and the lads—we saw it on the Internet. We weren't sure if it was you. But if it is—you were one of the youngest players ever to score a goal in the England under-nineteen team. And on your debut match,' Billy added breathlessly. 'And you scored that goal in the championship, the one that won the match.'

'It was a long time ago now. I haven't played in years,' Jared said.

Bailey couldn't quite work this out. Jared had been a star football player as a teenager? Then how come he was a doctor now? He didn't look that much older than she was—five years at the most, she reckoned—so surely he could still play football. Or, if he'd retired from football, it was more likely that he would have become a coach or a manager. Footballer to medic was quite a career change. Especially given that you needed four years at university followed by two years' foundation training, and then you had to work your way up the ranks. To be experienced enough to have a job as a football team doctor,

Jared must have been working in medicine for at least ten years. Maybe more. So why had he switched careers?

Feeling slightly guilty about being so nosy—but she could hardly ask the man himself, given how grumpy and impossible he was—she flicked onto the Internet on her phone and looked up 'Jared Fraser footballer England team' in a search engine.

The photograph was eighteen years old now, but the teenager was still recognisable as the man she knew. Jared Fraser had indeed been a footballer. One of the youngest players to score a goal for his country, at the age of seventeen. He'd played in several international matches and had scored the winning goal in a championship game. All the pundits had been tipping him to be one of the greatest players ever. But then, according to the online biography she was reading, he'd been involved in a bad tackle. One that had given him an anterior cruciate ligament injury that had ended his playing days.

So his dreams had been taken from him and

he'd ended up in a totally different career. Poor guy. It would, perhaps, explain the dourness. She'd be pretty grumpy, too, if she was no longer able to do her dream job.

Maybe she'd give Jared Fraser just a little bit of slack in future.

Though not from pity. She remembered what it felt like, being an object of pity. It was one of the reasons why she'd moved departments. She might've been able to stick it out, had it not been for the guilt—the knowledge that people felt they had to be careful around her instead of beaming their heads off about a piece of personal good news, the kind of joy everyone else would celebrate with. Because how did you tell someone you were expecting a baby when you knew they'd lost theirs, and in such a difficult way?

Yeah. Bailey Randall knew all about broken dreams. And how you just had to pick yourself up, dust yourself down and pretend that everything was absolutely fine. Because, if you did that, hopefully one day it *would* be just fine.

Halfway through the match, she noticed Travis lying on the ground, clutching his leg. Jared was already on his feet and running towards the boy; play had stopped and Jared was examining the player as she joined them.

'What's wrong?' she asked.

'Let me finish the SALTAPS stuff,' Jared said.

'SALTAPS?' It was obviously some kind of mnemonic, but not one she'd come across before.

'Stop play, analyse, look for injury, touch the site, active movement, passive movement, stand up,' he explained swiftly. 'Travis, what happened?'

'I don't know—there's just this pain down the back of my left leg,' the boy said, his face pale with pain.

Gently, Jared examined him. 'Did you hear a pop or a crack before the pain started?'

'I'm not sure,' Travis admitted. 'I was focusing on the ball.'

'OK. Does it hurt when you move?'

Travis nodded.

'I want you to bend your knee. If it hurts, stop moving straight away and tell me.'

The young player followed Jared's instructions and winced. 'It really hurts.'

'OK. I'm not even going to try the last bit—getting you up on your feet. I think you've got a hamstring injury, though I need to check a couple more things before I treat you. Archie's going to need to substitute you.'

'No, he can't!' Travis looked devastated. 'I'll be all right in a second or two. I'll be able to keep playing.'

Jared shook his head. 'Play on when you're injured and you'll do even more damage. You need treatment.'

Bailey had been pretty sure it was a hamstring injury, too, given Travis's symptoms. Hopefully it would be a partial rupture and wouldn't affect the whole muscle. 'Dr Fraser, you need to be on the pitch in case there's another injury,' she said. 'I'll take Travis to the dressing room and finish off the assessments for you.'

He looked at her and, for a moment, she thought he was going to refuse. Then he gave a brief nod. 'Thank you, Dr Randall. That would be helpful.'

'I'll talk to you when I've assessed him,' she said. Even though she was pretty sure that they'd recommend the same course of treatment, strictly speaking, Jared was in charge and Travis was his patient, and she was only here for research purposes. She didn't have the right to make decisions for Jared.

She supported Travis back to the dressing room. There was a wide, flat bench that would do nicely for her purposes; she gestured to it. 'OK. I want you to lie down here on your back, Travis, so I can go through the assessments and see how much damage you've done.'

'There's no need, really. I'll be all right in a few minutes,' Travis said, but she could see that his mouth was tight with pain.

'I still have to assess you, or Dr Fraser will have my guts for garters,' she said with a smile.

'OK. I'm going to raise your legs one at a time, keeping your knees straight. Tell me as soon as it hurts, OK? And I'll stop immediately.' She took him through a range of tests, noting his reactions.

'I'll put a compression bandage on—that'll stop the pain and the bleeding inside your ligament, which causes the inflammation—and an ice pack,' she said when she'd finished. 'And now I'm going to make you a cup of tea, and I want you to sit there with your leg up and the ice pack on the back of your thigh for the next ten minutes or so, while I go and talk to Dr Fraser, OK?'

'Yes, Doc.' He sighed. 'Am I going to be out of the team for long?'

'For at least a couple of weeks,' she said. 'I know it's hard and I know you want to play, but it's better to let yourself recover fully now than to play on it too soon and do more damage.' She finished making the tea. 'Sugar?'

'No. You're all right.' He gave her a rueful smile. 'Thanks, Doc.'

'That's what I'm here for. And painkillers,' she said. 'Are you allergic to anything, or taking any medication for anything?'

'No.'

'OK. I'll give you a couple of paracetamol for now—you can take some more in another four hours—and I'll see what else Dr Fraser suggests.' She patted his shoulder. 'Chin up. It could be worse.'

'Could it?' Travis asked, looking miserable.

'Oh, yes. Imagine having an itch on your leg in the middle of a really hot summer day—except your leg's in a full cast and you can't reach the itchy bit.'

That earned her another wry smile. 'OK. That's worse. Because I'd be off even longer with an actual break, wouldn't I?'

'Yes. But you're young and fit, so you'll heal just fine—as long as you do what Dr Fraser says.'

'I guess.'

She left him miserably sipping his mug of tea while she went to find Jared.

* * *

Jared knew the very moment that Bailey stepped out of the tunnel onto the field, even though his back was to her. The fact that he was so aware of her was slightly unnerving. They didn't even like each other—he'd known that even before she'd accidentally sent him that text saying exactly how she felt about him, in very unflattering terms. Dressed in a hooded sweatshirt, baggy tracksuit pants and flat training shoes, Bailey Randall should've looked slightly scruffy and absolutely unsexy—the complete opposite to his über-groomed ex-wife.

The problem was, Bailey was gorgeous. And those unflattering baggy clothes just made him want to peel them off and see exactly what was underneath them.

Not good. He didn't want to be attracted to her. He didn't want to be attracted to anyone.

Work, he reminded himself. This is work. You have an injured player, and she's helped you out. Be nice. Be polite. Be professional. And stay detached.

'How's young Travis?' he asked when she reached him.

'Pretty miserable,' she said.

Yeah. He knew how it felt, being taken off the pitch with an injury when you were desperate to keep playing. And, even though Travis's injury was relatively minor and he'd make a full recovery, Jared knew that the inactivity would make the boy utterly despondent. He'd been there himself. 'So what's your verdict?' he asked.

'I got him to do a straight leg raise and resisted knee flexion, then did a slump test and palpation,' she said. 'I'd say it's a grade two hamstring strain. I've put an ice pack on and a compression bandage for now and explained to him about standard RICE treatment. He's having a cup of tea while I'm talking to you and seeing what treatment you want him to have.'

'Thank you,' he said. He was impressed by the quiet, no-fuss way she'd examined the boy and reported back. There was no 'Told you so' or point-scoring against him, even though he probably deserved it; all her focus had been on making her patient comfortable. She'd also come to talk to him about a treatment plan instead of telling him how to treat his patient, despite the fact she was obviously more than capable of doing her own treatment plan, so she'd respected his position in the club, too. Maybe he'd been unfair to her about her project, because she'd been spot on about the actual medicine she'd discussed with him. If she was that competent, she was unlikely to be working on a project that had no merit.

'The poor lad's going to be gutted about missing training and matches, but he needs to do it properly or he'll end up with another tear in the muscle on top of this one, and it'll take even longer to heal,' she said.

Jared nodded. 'He needs cold therapy and compression every hour for the first day, and to keep his leg elevated while he's sitting, to reduce the swelling.'

'I gave him some paracetamol—he said he's

not on any other medication and he's not allergic to anything.'

'Good. That'll help with the pain during the acute stage, over the next couple of days,' he said.

'I told him that you'd come up with a rehab programme,' she said, 'but if he was my patient I'd suggest a sports massage at the end of the first week, and strengthening exercises in the meantime—standing knee flexion, bridge and seated hamstring curls with a resistance band. Nothing too strenuous, and he has to stop as soon as it hurts.'

'Good plan,' he said. Exactly what he would have suggested. They might not get on, but in medical terms they were definitely on the same page. 'He can also do some gentle walking and swimming, then introduce running gradually. Though it'll be several weeks before he's ready to come back to full training.'

She nodded. 'Look, I know you don't believe in the stuff I'm doing, and I'm not going to rub your nose in it and say "I told you so". But I do want some time to talk you through what I'm doing and—well, I suppose I really want to get you on board with the project,' she admitted. 'Can we have a meeting to talk about it—I mean *really* talk?'

If he'd listened to her and supported her argument that Travis was underperforming, the boy might not be sitting in the dressing room right now with a hamstring injury. Guilt made him sharp. 'The only free time I have is before breakfast.'

He knew he was being obnoxious, but he couldn't seem to stop himself. What was it about Bailey Randall that made him behave like this? Something about her just knocked him off balance, and he liked things to be in perfect equilibrium nowadays.

'Before breakfast,' she mused. 'I normally train at the gym then—but OK. I guess I can skip my session in the gym for once.'

'Or we could train in the gym together.' The words were out of his mouth before he could stop them. What on earth was wrong with him?

Panic flooded through him. This was *such* a bad idea.

'Train together, and then talk about my project over breakfast? That works for me. As long as your partner doesn't mind,' she added quickly.

'No partner.' Though he appreciated that she'd tried to be considerate. In the world of football, there was a lot of jealousy. Sasha definitely wouldn't have been happy about him having a breakfast meeting with a female colleague. Then again, Sasha had had meetings of her own with his male colleagues. In hotel rooms. He pushed the thought away. 'Will yours mind?' He tried to extend the same courtesy to Bailey.

'I'm single,' she said, 'and I like it that way.'

Which sounded to him as if she'd been hurt, too.

Not that it was any of his business. And he wouldn't dream of asking for details.

'One last thing to sort—my gym or yours?' she asked.

'So you don't go to a women-only gym?' Oh, great. And now he was insulting her.

She smiled. 'I'm not intimidated by anyone, regardless of their gender or their age or how pretty they are. I go to a place that has equipment I like and staff who can push me harder if I want a one-to-one training session. And it happens to be reasonably close to the London Victoria, so I can train before work.' She paused. 'There's a café there, too. The coffee's not brilliant, but they do a pretty good Eggs Florentine—which they don't serve in the hospital canteen, or I'd suggest breakfast there because their coffee's slightly better.'

There was no way he could back out of this now. 'OK. Your gym, tomorrow. Let me know the address and what time.'

'Seven,' she said. 'And I'll text you the address.' And there was a tiny, tiny hint of mischief in her eyes as she added, 'Herod.'

CHAPTER THREE

AT FIVE TO SEVEN the next morning, Jared walked down the street towards Bailey's gym. She was already waiting outside for him, wearing another of her hooded sweatshirts and baggy tracksuit pants, and she raised her hand to let him know she'd seen him. He acknowledged her with a nod.

'Good morning,' she said as he walked up to her. 'Are you ready for this?'

'Bring it on,' he said, responding to the challenge in her gaze and trying not to think about how gorgeous her mouth was. This was a challenge of sorts, not a date. They were supposed to be discussing business. And the fact that they were meeting here right now was his own fault—for being deliberately awkward and not trying to fit their meeting into normal working hours.

They walked into the reception, where she signed him in as her guest, and took him through to the changing rooms. 'I need to put my stuff in my locker. Meet you back outside here in five?'

'Sure.'

'Oh—and do you have a pound coin for your own locker? I have change if you need it.'

'Thanks, but I'm good.'

It didn't take him long to stow his things in the locker.

When Bailey came out from the women's changing rooms, Jared's jaw almost dropped. Clearly she'd been wearing the hoodie and the tracksuit pants just for warmth outside, because now she was wearing form-fitting black leggings and a bright cerise racer-back crop top. And he was horribly aware of just how gorgeous she was. Curvy, yet with fabulous muscle definition. Bailey Randall was a woman who looked after herself. She was utterly beautiful and could easily have held her own with any of the glamorous WAGs he'd known at the football clubs he'd worked at. And yet he didn't think she'd be the sort to go to endless spa days and nail parlours.

This was beginning to feel like the most enormous mistake. They were supposed to be training together and then discussing her project over breakfast, and all he wanted to do right now was to scoop her up and carry her to his bed. Even though it was actually a Tube ride away.

It was obvious that, like Sasha, Bailey was aware of her effect on men. She was gorgeous. So was Bailey like his ex-wife in using her physical attributes to get her own way? The idea made him pull himself together. Just. 'So what's your normal workout routine?' he asked.

'Today is a weights day,' she said, 'so that means a quick cardio warm-up and then a resistance routine. You?'

He shrugged. 'I'll join you and adjust the weights to suit me. Just tell me what we're doing and when.'

She nodded. 'Any injuries I should know about?'

Jared had no idea whether Archie had told her anything about his past, but it was irrelevant now. 'A very old knee problem,' he said. 'But I know my limits and I'm certainly not going to be stupid about it.'

'Good. Then let's do this. How about using the elliptical as a warm-up, then through into the back room with the free weights?'

'Fine by me.'

Why on earth had she agreed to train with him? Bailey asked herself. Jared was wearing baggy tracksuit pants and a loose sleeveless vest, like all the other men in the gym. She barely took any notice of them other than to smile hello, acknowledging the fellow athletes in her time slot. But Jared Fraser was different. She was horribly aware of the hard musculature of his body. Particularly his biceps.

He was an ex-footballer. A sports team doctor. He shouldn't have biceps that beautiful and that well defined.

Worst of all, she had a real thing about biceps.

Bailey always dragged Joni off to the cinema whenever her favourite actor had a new movie out—and Joni still teased Bailey about the time she'd said, 'Ohhh, just look at his biceps,' really loudly, in the middle of the cinema. The actor was incredibly handsome, perfectly built, but so was Jared Fraser.

She sneaked a sideways look. He was concentrating on putting the time and intensity settings into the elliptical machine, and right at that moment he looked incredibly sexy. It made her wonder what it would be like to have that brooding concentration completely focused on her, and she went hot all over. This training thing was a very bad move. She wished now that she hadn't challenged him. How on earth was she going to be able to concentrate on talking to him over breakfast? Even if he changed into something with long sleeves after his shower, she knew now that he had gorgeous biceps and that could seriously distract her. Right at that moment, she really wanted to reach over and touch him.

Well, she was going to have to make a lot more of an effort, because no way was she acting on that pull of attraction. She liked her life exactly as it was, with no complications—and Jared Fraser could be a real complication. If she let him. Which she really didn't intend to do.

When they'd finished warming up, Bailey talked him through her planned routine, the large compound movements that worked several muscle groups at once. 'I thought I'd do a full-body workout today, if that's OK with you, rather than an upper or lower split.'

'It's a good balance,' he said. 'I notice you're doing hams and then quads.'

'You need to balance them out properly or you'll end up with a back injury,' she said, 'and you wouldn't believe how many patients I have to explain that to.'

Funny how easy it was to talk to him when they were both concentrating on doing the right number of reps and keeping their form correct.

'What made you specialise in sports medicine?' he asked.

'I started off in emergency medicine,' she said, 'but then I found myself doing more of the sporting injuries, especially at the weekends or on Monday mornings. I did think about maybe working in orthopaedics, but then again I like the preventative stuff, too—it's great being able to make a difference. Then I had the chance of a secondment in the new sports medicine department. I liked my colleagues and I liked the work, so I stayed.'

That was the brief version. She had no intention of telling Jared the rest of it—how that secondment had saved her sanity, just over two years ago, and given her something else to concentrate on when she'd desperately needed an escape. OK, so in sports medicine there wasn't the speed and pressure that could take her mind off things as there was in the emergency department; but she also didn't have to walk into her department again after first-hand experience of being treated there, knowing that everyone in the department knew exactly what had happened to her and trying to avoid the concern that shaded too far into pity.

'What about you?' she asked. 'Why did you become the doctor of a football team?'

She wondered if he was going to tell her about his past as a footballer, but he merely said, 'I enjoy working in sports medicine, and this job means I get to travel a bit.'

Surely he must've guessed that she'd looked him up and knew what had happened to his knee? Then again, it had been a life-changing accident, and he was on a completely different path now. She didn't blame him for not wanting to talk about the injury that had wrecked his career—just as she didn't want to talk about the ectopic pregnancy that had shattered her dreams and then cracked her marriage beyond repair. No doubt he, too, knew what it felt like to be sick and tired of pity. They didn't have to discuss it.

'How did you get involved in this research project, or have you always been a football fan?' he asked.

'I ought to admit that I'd much rather do sport than watch it, and football isn't really top of my list,' she said. 'My boss was asked if someone on his team would work on the project, and he thought I'd enjoy it because...' She felt her face heat. 'Well, I like techie stuff,' she confessed. 'A lot.'

'You mean gadgets?' He zeroed in on exactly the thing she knew he'd pick up on. 'And would I be right in guessing that you've got one of those expensive wristband things?'

'Um, yes,' she admitted. 'I use it all the time in the gym. I didn't wear it today simply because I knew you'd be really rude about it.'

He burst out laughing. It was the first time she'd actually heard him laugh and it was gorgeous, rich and deep. Sexy, even. *Oh, help.*

'Oh, come off it—are you trying to tell me that you don't like game consoles and whatever?' she asked. 'My brothers are total addicts and so are Joni's—my best friend,' she explained.

'I'm not so much into game consoles,' he

said, 'but I do like music—and that's where my techie stuff comes in. I bought one of those systems where the sound follows you through the house.' Then he looked surprised, as if he hadn't meant to tell her something so personal.

'What kind of music?' she asked.

'What do you think?' he parried.

She looked at him as she put the barbell down. 'I'd say either dinosaur rock or very highbrow classical.'

'The first,' he said.

She almost—*almost*—told him about Joni's brother's band and invited him along to their next gig. But that would be too much like asking him out on a date. She and Jared Fraser most definitely weren't on dating terms.

'I'm assuming you like the stuff you can sing along to,' he said.

'Musicals,' she said. 'I'm pretty much word perfect on the soundtracks to *Grease*, *Cats* and *Evita*.'

'Uh-huh.'

But there was a tiny hint of superciliousness

in his expression, so she added, 'And Dean Martin. Nonno's favourite. He taught me all the famous songs when I was tiny—"That's Amore", "Volare" and "Sway".' Just in case Jared had any intention of mocking *that*, she said, 'And, actually, it's great stuff to salsa to. It's not old-fashioned at all.'

'Nonno?' he asked, looking confused.

'My grandfather in Milan. My mum is Italian,' she said.

'That explains it.'

'Explains what?' She narrowed her eyes at him.

'Why I thought you were a bit like a pampered Mediterranean princess when I first met you.' Then he looked really horrified, as if he hadn't meant to say that.

'A pampered princess,' she said, and glowered at him. 'You think I'm *spoiled*?'

He stretched out a foot and prodded the floor next to the mats. 'Ah. The floor's obviously not going to open up and swallow me.'

It amused her, though at the same time she

was a bit annoyed at what he was implying. 'Princess,' she said again in disgust.

'Hey. You called me Herod,' he pointed out.

'That was an autocorrect thing on my phone, and it wasn't meant for you in any case. You know what they say about eavesdroppers hearing no good of themselves,' she said loftily.

'You didn't actually take it back, though,' he reminded her.

'No, I didn't—I do think you have tyrant tendencies,' she said, 'given how you wouldn't even listen to what Archie or I said about the project.' She paused. 'And the fact that you could dismiss me as princessy just now, when you barely even know me. That's definitely Herod-like behaviour.'

'I think,' he said, 'we just got back onto the wrong foot with each other—and this morning's meant to be about listening to each other's point of view and finding a bit of common ground.'

He had a point. Maybe she should cut him some slack. 'So you're actually going to listen to what I say? And you'll admit that you were wrong about Travis?'

'*Possibly* wrong,' he corrected. 'That injury might still have happened to one of the other players—one who was performing around his normal average on your charts.'

It was much less likely, she thought. But at least he was admitting the possibility that he was wrong. That was a start. 'What about the yoga?' she challenged.

'No. I'm not convinced. At all,' he said.

'So you think yoga is easy?'

'It's simple stretching.'

Remembering the conversation she'd had with Joni, Bailey smiled. 'Right. So we can finish this session with a bit of yoga, then.'

He rolled his eyes, but muttered, 'If you must.'

When they'd finished the weights routine, she said, 'Yoga will be the cool down and stretch. Have you ever done any before?'

He stared at her. 'Do I look as if I do yoga?'

'Actually, there are a couple of men in our class. They recognise the importance of flexibility training as part of a balanced exercise programme,' she pointed out. 'But OK. I'll talk you through the poses.' First, she talked him through the downward dog. She noticed that he seemed reasonably flexible, and she was impressed that he managed both the warrior pose and the tree without any difficulty. He had a strong core, then.

'So far, so easy?' she asked.

'I can tell which muscle groups each one works,' he said.

'Good. Now for the plank,' she said, and showed him the position. She moved so she could see the clock. 'And we'll start in five. Hold it for as long as you can.' She counted them down, then they both assumed the position.

Jared managed to hold it for a minute before he flopped.

Bailey took it to three—even though that was pushing it, for her—just to make the point.

It looked effortless, though Jared could see Bailey's arms just beginning to shake and he knew that her muscles were right on the verge of giving in. But, when she stopped the pose, he knew he was going to have to be gracious about it—especially given that her performance had been so much better than his.

'OK,' he said, 'I admit that was hard. And clearly you've done that particular one a lot.'

She grinned. 'I have. That one usually shuts people up when they say yoga's an easy option. Though, actually, you did well. A lot of people cave after twenty seconds, or even before that.'

He appreciated the compliment, particularly as it sounded genuine and as if she was trying to meet him halfway.

'So you do a lot of yoga?' he asked.

'Every Monday night with my best friend. Any decent training regime needs flexibility work as well as resistance and cardio.'

He agreed with that. 'So what do you do for cardio?'

She actually blushed.

And he started to have all kinds of seriously impure thoughts about her. He really wished he hadn't started this discussion. The fact that she'd blushed meant she must be thinking something similar. So the attraction was mutual, then? Heat zinged through him. If she felt the same pull, what did that mean?

Then again, he didn't want to get involved with anyone. Sasha had hurt him badly—not just with the affair, but the bit she'd really lied to him about—and Jared wasn't sure he was ready to trust again.

'Cardio. I like dance-based classes,' she said. 'Also there's a salsa night at a local club. I quite often go to that. I like the music, and the dancing's fun. I'm a great believer in endorphins.'

For a moment Jared thought she was going to challenge him to go with her—and he wasn't sure if he was more relieved or disappointed when she didn't. He'd hated clubbing with Sasha in any case; a salsa club was probably just as much of a meat market as any other kind of dance club, and that didn't really appeal to him. Though the idea of dancing with Bailey Randall, up close, hot and sweaty, with her body pressed against his…

Focus, he told himself. Work, not sex.

'I assume you run?' she asked.

'Intervals,' he said, 'and rowing—it's more effective than hamster-wheel cardio. No offence to your warm-up today, because that was fine—it's just that it would bore me stupid if it lasted for more than ten minutes, even with a decent playlist to keep me going.'

'Each to their own,' she said. 'I don't mind doing a whole session on the elliptical if I have a good playlist. There are programmes on the machine that change the resistance and make it a bit more interesting.'

He just grimaced.

'So, rowing, hmm? That would explain your biceps.'

And then she blushed again.

Now he was really intrigued. She liked his biceps?

Well, he liked the muscles in her back. They had beautiful definition. And he really, really wanted to touch them. No. More than that. He wanted to kiss his way down her spine.

'Would that be proper rowing on a river, or machine?' she asked.

'Machine,' he admitted.

'And I assume you're careful with your knee.'

'I'm wearing a knee support under my track-suit pants,' he said. 'I'm hardly going to nag my players about looking after themselves properly and then not take my own advice.'

'I guess.' She held out her hand to shake his, and his palm tingled where their skin touched. How long had it been since he'd been so aware of someone? 'That was a good session. I enjoyed working with you, Jared.'

'I enjoyed working with you,' he said, meaning it; he was surprised to realise just how much he'd enjoyed it.

'Let's hit the shower and have breakfast.'

He went hot all over again at the thought of sharing a shower with her. He knew perfectly well that wasn't what she'd meant, but now the idea was stuck in his head. And he was glad they had temperature settings on the showers in the male changing rooms, because he needed a blast of cold water to get his common sense back and the fantasies out of his mind.

When he met Bailey outside the changing rooms, he noticed that she was wearing a black tailored suit for work. This was yet another side of her; he'd seen the slightly scruffy scientist on the football pitch and the sculpted goddess in the gym, and now she was the calm, confident medical professional.

He wished that he was wearing something a bit more tailored, too—but then again he was off to work himself after this and that meant dressing appropriately. A sharp suit wasn't what you needed when you were working on a football pitch.

Clearly the staff knew Bailey well here, because the waitress didn't bat an eyelid when Bailey ordered Eggs Florentine without the hollandaise sauce. 'And a rich roast latte?' the waitress asked.

It was obviously Bailey's usual, because she smiled. 'That'd be lovely, thanks.'

He ordered porridge with blueberries and cinnamon, paired with a protein shake.

'Not a coffee fiend?' she asked.

'I had mine before my workout. It gets the best use out of the caffeine,' he said. 'I'm balancing my protein and my carbs now, post-workout.'

She nodded. 'Good point.'

'So, are you going to take me through this system of yours while we wait for breakfast to arrive?'

'Sure. The idea behind it is that you're more likely to end up with a soft-tissue injury if you play while you're under par. You'll be slower and your reactions won't be as fast. So if you look at your performance during training or a game and your VO2 is down, you're doing fewer steps, your resting heart rate is up and your average speed is down, either you've had a slow game—and that's where Archie comes in, to tell me if playing conditions on the field have been different and affected anyone's performance—or you're under par and you're more likely to be injured in your next game.'

He asked her various questions about the measurements she used, and he was impressed that she didn't have to look up a single answer. Bailey Randall wasn't the glib salesman type, able to put a spin on her answers; she really knew her stuff. And she clearly believed in her research project. He liked her enthusiasm; it was one of the reasons why he'd chosen to look after the youth team, because he loved the enthusiasm that young players brought to the job, unjaded by internal politics.

And he also liked the way Bailey talked with her hands, completely animated when she was caught up in the subject. Now he knew she was half-Italian, he could really see it. Everything from her classic bone structure, to the slightly olive colour of her skin, to the rich depths of her eyes. Naturally stylish, she was like an Italian Audrey Hepburn, with that gamine haircut and those huge eyes.

'OK,' he said. 'I still think those wristband

things are ploys to extort money out of the gullible with too much disposable income and too little common sense, but the stuff you're doing has a point.'

'Thank you,' she said. 'So do you take it back about my system being a glorified pedometer?'

'I'll reserve judgement until I've seen a month of results,' he said, 'but I will agree that it's better than the wristband things. Especially because you do at least use a proper heart-rate monitor strap with your system.'

'And the yoga?'

He shook his head. 'Even though the plank was hard, I'm not convinced that yoga's going to do what you think it will. Not for a bunch of seventeen-year-old boys.'

'It's still worth a try.'

'Do you make them do the plank?'

She laughed. 'No. That was just to prove a point to you.'

He liked the fact that she'd admitted it.

And it worried him that he liked it. Now that he was getting to know her, he quite liked Bailey Randall. Which was a very dangerous position. He couldn't afford to think of her in terms of anything other than a colleague, but she seriously tempted him. To the point where he could actually imagine asking her out on a date.

Bad, bad move.

He had a feeling that he was going to have to resort to a lot of cold showers to keep his common sense in place. Dating Bailey Randall was absolutely not on the cards. He'd only just finished gluing the pieces of his heart back together, and he had no intention of putting himself back in a position where it could shatter again.

CHAPTER FOUR

OVER THE NEXT couple of weeks, working at the football club was easier, Bailey thought. Jared was at least showing some interest in her research project rather than being an insurmountable bulwark, and he'd even come up with a couple of suggestions that she was trying to incorporate into her data.

Then she noticed that he was favouring his right knee when he went onto the pitch to treat one of the players. She waited until he'd come back to sit next to her on the bench, and then asked, 'What did you do?'

'For Mitch?' He shrugged. 'It was just a flesh wound—some studs scraped against his shin, so I cleaned it and dressed it. He shouldn't have too much trouble with it.'

'No, I meant what did you do to your knee?'

He looked away. 'Nothing.'

'Jared, I'm a doctor, so don't try to flannel me. I could see you were favouring your right knee,' she said.

He sighed. 'It's an old injury. I guess I might have overdone the running a tad at the weekend.'

'Tsk. And you're a sports medicine doctor,' she said.

He gave her a crooked grin that made her libido sit up and beg. 'It'll be fine. It's strapped up.'

'So you didn't actually see anyone about it?'

'I didn't need to.'

She tutted. 'What a fine example to set the team—*not*. Let me have a look when they've gone, so they don't know what an idiot you are.'

He shook his head. 'It's fine. You don't have to do that.'

'You're my colleague. You'd do the same for me.'

Jared thought about it. Would he? Yes, probably. And he'd nag her if she was being stubborn about it, just as he'd nag Archie. Just as she was nagging him. 'I guess,' he admitted.

'Are you icing it? Because obviously you're not resting it or elevating it.'

'No. I'm taking painkillers,' he said. 'And not strong ones, either. Just normal ibuprofen to deal with the inflammation.'

'Hmm,' she said.

After the training session, Jared said to Archie, 'I'll lock up if you need to go. I want to discuss a couple of things with Dr Randall.'

'Cheers,' Archie said. 'It'll give me a few extra minutes to make myself beautiful for my date.'

'What, another one?' Bailey teased. 'I'm sure she'll think you look beautiful.' She blew him a kiss.

Archie grinned and sketched a bow.

'Why didn't you just tell him that your knee hurts?' Bailey asked quietly when Archie and the players had gone, and she and Jared were alone in the dressing room.

'Because it isn't relevant.'

'Of course it's relevant. If you have to kneel on the pitch to treat one of the players, it's going to hurt you.' She rolled her eyes. 'Men.'

'Women,' he sniped back.

'Just shut up and lose the tracksuit bottoms.'

Oh, help. The pictures that put into his head. To clear them, he drawled, 'Fabulous bedside manner, Dr Randall.'

Except that made it worse. Bed. Bailey. Two words he really shouldn't have put together inside his head, because now he could imagine her lying against his pillows and giving him a come-hither smile…

She just gave him a dry look. He shut up and removed his tracksuit bottoms. He knew she wasn't thinking of him in terms of a man right now, but in terms of a patient. What she saw wasn't six foot two of man; she saw a sore knee. An old injury playing up that needed to be looked at and soothed.

Gently she examined his knee. 'Tell me where it hurts, and don't be stubborn about it—because I can't help you if you're not honest with me.'

'Do you talk to all your patients like this?' he asked.

'Just the awkward ones.'

He guessed he deserved that. 'OK. It hurts there. And there.' He gave a sharp intake of breath. 'And there.'

'All righty.' She grabbed a towel and spread it across her lap. 'Leg. Here. Now.'

His bare leg astride her body.

Uh-oh. How on earth was he meant to stop his thoughts doing a happy dance?

'Yes, ma'am,' he drawled, hoping she didn't have a clue what was going through his head right now.

Her hands had been gentle when she'd examined his knee. Now they were firm. There wasn't anything remotely sexual about the way she touched him, and he had to grit his teeth on more than one occasion.

But when she'd finished the deep-tissue massage, he could move an awful lot more easily.

'You're very good at that,' he said when she'd

finished and he'd put his tracksuit bottoms back on. 'Thank you.'

'Better?' she asked.

He nodded. 'Sorry for being snippy with you.'

She shrugged. 'You were in pain. Of course you were going to be snippy. It's forgotten.'

'Thanks. I owe you one,' he said lightly, expecting her to brush it aside.

To his surprise, she looked thoughtful. 'I wonder.'

'Wonder what?'

'I do need a favour, actually, and you'd be perfect.'

He still wasn't following this. 'For what?'

She took a deep breath. 'My best friend's getting married in three weeks' time. And I'm under a bit of pressure to take someone to the wedding with me. My family's convinced that I need someone in my life, and I can't get them to see that I'm perfectly happy just concentrating on my career.'

'You want me to go to a wedding with you?'

'Yes.'

'As your partner?'

She grimaced. 'I'm not asking you on a date, Jared. I'm asking you to do me a favour.'

'To be your pretend boyfriend.'

'For one day. And an evening,' she added.

Go with her to a wedding.

She'd just made his knee feel a lot better. And this would be payback.

But…a *wedding*.

Where people promised to love, honour and cherish, until death did them part.

Vows he'd taken himself, and had meant every single word—although it turned out that Sasha hadn't. For all he knew, Tom hadn't even been her first affair. He'd been so clueless, thinking that his wife was happy, when all the time she'd been looking for something else.

Sasha had broken every single one of her vows.

She'd lied, she'd cheated—and then she'd made a crucial decision without talking it over with him. A decision that had cut Jared to the quick because he really couldn't understand her reasoning and it was totally the opposite of what he'd wanted. Even *if* the baby hadn't been his, it would still have been hers. They could've worked something out.

Except she hadn't wanted to. The only person she'd thought about had been herself. Not him, not the baby, not the other man who also might've been the baby's father—as she'd been sleeping with them both, she'd had no idea who the father of her baby was.

To go and celebrate someone else making those same vows when he'd lost his faith in marriage…that would be hard.

'If it's a problem…' her voice was very cool '…then forget I asked.'

He didn't want to tell Bailey about the mess of his divorce, Sasha's betrayal and the termination. He didn't want her to pity him. Besides, he owed her for helping him with his knee. 'OK. I'll do it.'

He knew it sounded grudging, and her raised eyebrow confirmed it. He sighed. 'Sorry. I didn't mean to sound quite so—well—Herod-ish.'

That netted him the glimmer of a smile. 'Knee still hurting?' she asked.

It would be an easy excuse. But he thought she deserved the truth. 'Let's just say I've seen a lot of divorces.' He'd been through a messy one, too. Not that she needed to know that bit. 'So I guess my view of weddings is a bit dark.'

'This one,' Bailey said, 'is definitely going to work. My best friend used to be engaged to a total jerk, but thankfully she realised how miserable her life was going to be with him, and she called it off.'

Interesting. So Bailey was a realist rather than seeing things through rose-tinted glasses? 'I take it you like the guy she's marrying?'

She nodded. 'Aaron's a genuinely nice guy. And he loves Joni as much as she loves him. It's equal.'

Did that mean Bailey had been in a relationship that hadn't been equal, or was he reading too much into this?

'Plus,' she said, 'I happen to know the food's going to be good—and the music. Joni's brother has a band, and they're playing at the evening do.' She paused. 'Dinosaur rock. They're seriously good. So I think you'll enjoy that.'

'You don't need to sell it to me. I've already said I'll go with you, and I keep my word.'

Funny how brown eyes could suddenly seem so piercing. And then she nodded. 'Yes. You have integrity. It's better to be grumpy with integrity than to be charming and unreliable.'

That *definitely* sounded personal. And it intrigued him. But if he asked her any more, then she'd be able to ask him things he'd rather not answer. 'Let me know when and where the plus-one thing is, then,' he said instead.

'Thanks. I will.'

Bailey couldn't stop thinking about Jared on the way home. The world of football was pretty high profile—as much as the worlds of music and Hollywood were—and the gossip magazines were forever reporting divorces and affairs among sporting stars. But something in Jared's expression had made her think that it was a bit more personal than that. Was Jared divorced? Not that she'd pry and ask him. But it made her feel a bit as if she'd railroaded him into agreeing to be her partner at the wedding. And that wasn't fair.

When she got home, she texted him: You really *don't* have to go to the wedding.

The answer came back promptly: I said I'd do it. I'll keep my word.

Typical Jared. Stubborn.

Well, she'd given him the chance to back out. But hopefully he wouldn't hate it as much as he seemed to think he would. OK, thanks, she texted back, and added all the details of the wedding.

The next day was one of Bailey's clinic days at the London Victoria. Her first patient was a teenager who'd been injured playing tennis.

'Viv landed awkwardly in training,' Mr Kaine said. 'She said she felt her knee give and heard a popping sound. And her knee's started to swell really badly.' He indicated his daughter's knee. 'It hurts to walk.'

'It's just a sprain, Dad. It'll be fine,' Vivienne said. 'Let's stop wasting the doctor's time and go home.'

'No,' he said firmly. 'You're going to get this checked out *properly*.'

It sounded as if Mr Kaine was putting his daughter's welfare first and would support her through any treatment programme—which was a good thing, Bailey thought, because what he'd just described sounded very like the injury that had finished Jared's career. Damage to the anterior cruciate ligament.

She pushed Jared to the back of her mind. Not here, not now. Her patient came first.

'Thank you for giving me the background, Mr Kaine. That's very useful,' she said cheerfully. 'Vivienne, would you mind if I examine your knee?' she asked.

The girl rolled her eyes, as if she thought this was a total waste of time, but nodded. She flinched when Bailey touched her knee, so clearly it hurt to the touch and Bailey was very, very gentle as she finished examining the girl's knee.

'I'm going to send you for an MRI scan to confirm it,' she said, 'but I'm fairly sure you've torn your anterior cruciate ligament. I'm afraid you're going to be out of play for a little while.'

Again, she thought of Jared. He must have had a similar consultation with a doctor at a very similar age.

'What? But I *have* to play! I've got an important tournament next week,' Vivienne said, looking horrified. 'I've been training for months. I can't miss it!'

However bad the girl felt about it, she had to face up to the severity of her injury. She wouldn't even be able to have a casual knockabout on the court for a while, let alone play an important match on the junior tennis circuit. Not even if her knee was strapped up.

'Viv, you have to listen to the doctor. She knows what she's talking about,' Mr Kaine said. 'I'm sorry, Dr Randall. You were explaining to us what Vivienne's done to her knee.'

Bailey drew a couple of diagrams to show Vivienne how the ligaments worked and what had happened to her knee. 'You have a complete tear of the ligament—it's the most common type, and I'm afraid it also means you've damaged the other ligaments and your cartilage.'

'Will it take long to fix?' Vivienne asked. 'If I miss this tournament, can I play in the next one?'

'I'm afraid that's unlikely,' Bailey said. 'You're going to need surgery.'

'Surgery?' The girl looked totally shocked. 'But—but—that means I'll be out for ages!'

'The injury won't heal on its own and unfortunately you can't just stitch a ligament back together. Vivienne, I'll need to send you to a specialist surgeon. I know Dr Martyn here quite well, and he's really good at his job, so I promise you'll be in the best hands.' She looked up at Vivienne's father and gave him a reassuring smile, too. 'He'll replace your torn ligament with a tissue graft, which will act as a kind of scaffolding for the new ligament to grow on. You'll be on crutches for a while afterwards.'

'Crutches. I can't play tennis with *crutches*.' Vivienne shook her head. 'This can't be happening. It just can't.'

'Crutches will stop you putting weight on your leg and damaging the structure of your knee further,' Bailey said. 'I can also give you a brace to protect your knee and make it more stable. But I'm afraid it's going to be at least six months until you can play sports again. After the surgery, you'll need a rehab physiotherapy programme—that means exercises tailored to strengthen your leg muscles and make your knee functional again.'

'Six months.' Vivienne closed her eyes. 'Oh, my God. My life's over.'

'Viv, it's going to take six months for you to get better. I know it feels bad, but it's not the end of the world. You'll come back stronger,' Mr Kaine said.

It was good that her dad was so supportive,

Bailey thought. But Vivienne was clearly finding it hard to adjust.

'If you go back to playing too soon, you might do more damage to your knee and you'll be out of action for a lot longer,' Bailey said. 'The good news is that the way they do surgery today is a lot less invasive. It's keyhole surgery, so that means you'll have less pain, you'll spend less time in hospital and you'll recover more quickly.'

'When will the surgeon do it?' Mr Kaine asked. 'Today? Tomorrow?'

'Not straight away,' Bailey said. 'We need the inflammation to go down a bit first, or there's a risk of scar tissue forming inside the joint and you'll lose part of your range of motion.'

'And that means I won't be able to play tennis the way I do now.' Vivienne bit her lip. 'Not ever.'

'Exactly,' Bailey said. 'What you do next is going to make the biggest difference. For the next seventy-two hours you need to remember RICE—rest, ice, compression and elevation.'

She talked Vivienne through the treatment protocols.

'What about a hot-water bottle to help with the pain?' Mr Kaine asked.

Bailey shook her head. 'Not for the first three days—and no alcohol, either.'

Vivienne rolled her eyes. 'Fat chance of that. Dad's part of the food police. We were told in sixth form that as soon as you're sixteen you're allowed a glass of wine with your meal in a restaurant. But Dad won't let me.'

'Alcohol slows your reactions and you can't play tennis with a hangover,' he said. 'At least, not well—and I should know because I've tried it.'

Bailey smiled at him. He was definitely going to need a sense of humour to help coax Vivienne through the next few months of a total ban from tennis. 'No running or massage, either,' she said. 'But I can give you painkillers—ones that will help reduce the inflammation as well as the pain.' She looked at Mr Kaine. 'Are there any allergies I need to know about?'

'No,' he confirmed.

'Good.'

'Six months,' Vivienne said again, making it sound like a life sentence.

'Better to make up a bit of ground in a couple of months,' Bailey said softly, 'than to go back too soon, do more damage and then have to spend even more time recovering.'

'She's right, love.' Mr Kaine rested his hand briefly on his daughter's shoulder. 'So what happens after the operation?'

'For the first three weeks the physio will concentrate on increasing the range of motion in the joint but without ripping the graft,' Bailey said. 'By week six Vivienne should be able to use a stair-climber or a stationary bike to maintain the range of motion and start strengthening her muscles, and then the plan will be to work to full rehab over the next few months. You need a balance between doing enough to rehabilitate the knee,' she said gently to Vivienne, 'but not so much that you damage the surgical repair and make the ligament fail again.'

'Six months,' Vivienne said again, looking totally miserable.

'There are other things you can work on that won't involve your knee,' Mr Kaine said cheerfully. 'Chin up.'

Vivenne just sighed.

Once Bailey had sorted out a compression bandage and painkillers, she said, 'I'll see you again in a couple of days and then we'll see the surgeon. Reception will make an appointment for you. Call me if you're worried about anything. But we'll get your knee fixed and you'll be back to playing tennis again.'

And, some time before their next appointment, there was someone she needed to talk to who might just be able to give her some really, really good advice to help Vivienne cope with the next few months.

She hoped.

CHAPTER FIVE

THERE WAS NEVER going to be a perfect time
to ask Jared, Bailey knew, and she certainly
wasn't going to ring him outside office hours
to talk it through with him. But once the next
training session with the team was under way
and she was seated on the bench next to him,
she turned to him.

'Can I ask you for some professional advice—
something that's a bit personal?'

He looked completely taken aback. 'Why?'

She'd known before she asked that this was
going to be difficult; Jared had never talked to
her about his injury. But he was the only one
who might be able to help. 'I have a patient, a
teenage female tennis player. She landed awkwardly from hitting a ball.'

'And?'

'She, um, has a complete tear to her ACL.'

He went very, very still and guilt flooded through her.

'I know I'm being intrusive,' she said, 'and I apologise for that. I really don't mean to dredge up bad memories for you about your own injury. And, yes, I did look you up, so I know what happened. I could hardly ask you, could I?'

'I guess not.'

Talk about inscrutable. Jared's voice and his face were completely expressionless, so she had absolutely no idea how he was feeling right now. Worrying that she was risking their newfound truce, but wanting to get some real help for her patient, she said, 'The reason I'm asking you is because when it happened you were about the same age as she is now, so you know how it feels. Her dad's really supportive and he's trying to get her to rest her knee sensibly so she'll recover well from the operation, but she's distraught at the idea that she's going to lose a lot of ground over the next year. So I guess what I'm asking you is if there's anything I can tell her to help her deal with it a bit better.'

For a moment she thought Jared was going to blank her, but then he blew out a breath. 'That really depends on whether she's going to recover fully or not.'

Clearly he hadn't recovered fully enough to be able to resume his sports career. But she knew that if she tried to give him a hug—out of empathy rather than pity—he'd push her away, both literally and figuratively. So she kept the topic to a discussion about her patient. 'I think there's a very good chance she'll recover fully. The surgeon's brilliant,' Bailey said.

'Good.'

A complete tear to the anterior cruciate ligament. Jared knew exactly how that felt. Like the end of the world. When all your dreams had suddenly exploded and there wasn't any meaning in your life any more. You couldn't do the one thing you knew you were really good at— the thing you were born to do. In a few moments it was all gone.

At seventeen, it had destroyed him. Knowing that his knee wouldn't hold up in the future—that if he played again he was likely to do more damage to his knee and eventually he'd be left with a permanent limp. Knowing that he'd never play for his country again. He'd been so sure that nothing would ever be that good for the rest of his life.

Although it hadn't actually turned out that way. He enjoyed his job, and he was still involved with the game he loved.

He blew out a breath. 'It's a lot to deal with. Especially at that age. Tell her to take it one day at a time, and to find someone she can talk to. Someone who won't let her wallow in self-pity and will talk her into being sensible.' He'd been so, so lucky that the team's deputy coach had been brilliant with him. He'd let Jared rant and rave, and then told him to look at his options, because there most definitely *would* be something he could do.

What goes around comes around. It was time to pass on that same advice now. 'Tell her there will be something else. At first it'll feel like second best, but she'll find something else she loves as much. Even if it doesn't look like it right now.'

'Thank you,' Bailey said quietly. 'I appreciate it—and I'm sorry I brought back bad memories. That really wasn't my intention.'

He shrugged again. 'It was a long time ago.'

She said nothing, simply waited, and he was surprised to find himself filling in the gap. 'At the time, it was bad,' he admitted. 'I wanted someone to blame for the end of my dreams—but I always knew that the tackle wasn't deliberate. It was just something that went wrong and it could've happened to anyone. The guy who tackled me felt as guilty as hell about it, but it wasn't his fault. It wasn't anyone's fault. It was just an accident. Wrong time, wrong place.' He paused. 'And I found something else to do.'

'Did you think about coaching?' She put a hand across her mouth. 'Sorry. You don't have to answer that.'

He liked the fact that she wasn't pressuring him. There was no malice in Bailey Randall.

She just wanted to help her patient, and he'd had first-hand experience of what her patient was going through right now. Of course she'd want to know how he'd coped. 'I thought about it,' he said. 'Though I knew I was too young to be taken seriously when my knee was wrecked. At seventeen, you don't really have enough experience to coach a team.'

'So why did you choose medicine? That's— well, a huge change of direction.'

'My family are all GPs,' he said. 'I'd always thought I'd join them. I guess it was a surprise to everyone when I was spotted on the playing field at school and the local team took me on for training.' He shrugged. 'Then I had to make a choice. Risk trying for a career in football, or do my A-levels. My parents said to give it a go—I could always take my A-levels later if it didn't work out. And when I was picked for the England squad…they threw one hell of a party.'

He smiled at the memory. 'When my knee went, it hit me pretty hard. But I was lucky in a way, in that I could fall back on my original

plans—I just took my A-levels two years later
than I would've done if I hadn't tried for a career in sport.'

'So you trained as a GP?' she asked.

'No. I ended up training in emergency medicine,' he said. 'I liked the buzz. Then, like you,
I had a secondment to a sports medicine department. And then it occurred to me that I could
have the best of both worlds—I could be a doctor in the sport I'd always loved.'

'That's a good compromise,' she said.

Again, to his surprise, he found himself asking questions and actually wanting to know the
answers rather than being polite. 'What about
you? Is your family in medicine?'

'No—my family has a restaurant. Mum's the
head chef, Dad's front of house and my brothers
are both kitchen serfs.' At Jared's raised eyebrows, she added swiftly, 'Joke. Gio is Mum's
deputy—he's going to take over when she re-
tires. And Rob's probably the best pastry chef
in the universe and he makes the most amazing

wedding cakes. They're planning to expand the business that way, too.'

'Didn't your parents expect you to join the family firm?'

She shook her head. 'Mum and Dad always said that we should follow our hearts and do what we love, and that they'd back us whatever we decided. Rob and Gio were always in the kitchen making stuff, so it was obvious what they wanted to do. And I was always bandaging my teddies when I was a toddler.' She grinned. 'And the dog, if I could get him to sit still.'

He could just imagine that. He'd bet she'd been the most determined and stubborn toddler ever. 'A born doctor, then?'

'I've no idea where it came from. It was just what I always wanted to do,' she said. 'And I guess I was lucky because my family's always supported me. Even when I nag them about healthy eating and saturated fat.' She laughed. 'Though the nagging has at least made them put some super-healthy options on the menu—that's gone down really well with the customers, so

I feel I've made some kind of contribution to the family business, apart from volunteering to taste-test any new stuff.'

Clearly Bailey was very close to her family and Jared had a feeling that they adored her as much as she obviously adored them. And she cared enough about her patients to do something outside her comfort zone; he knew that it must've been daunting to ask him about the injury he didn't talk about, but she'd asked him to see if he could help her patient rather than because she wanted to pry into his life.

'Your patient,' he said. 'When are you seeing her next?'

'Friday morning.'

'I could,' he suggested, 'come and have a word with her, if you like.'

'Really?' The way she smiled at him made him feel as if the sun had just come out at midnight.

'It might help her to talk to someone who's been there and come out just fine on the other side,' he said.

'I think it would help her a lot. If you're sure.' She bit her lip. 'I mean, I don't want to rip open any old scars.'

He smiled. 'It was a long time ago now. And I was lucky—I had someone who helped me. It's my chance to pay it forward.'

She rested a hand on his arm; even through his sleeve, her touch made his skin tingle. 'Thank you, Jared. I really appreciate it.'

'No worries,' he said.

On Friday, Bailey saw Vivienne in her clinic at the London Victoria and examined her knee. 'Obviously you've followed my advice about rest, ice, compression and elevation,' she said.

Vivienne nodded. 'I want to play again as soon as possible. That means doing what you say.'

Bailey smiled. 'Well, you'll be pleased to know you're good to go for surgery and you can see the surgeon this afternoon.'

'That's great news,' Mr Kaine said, patting his daughter's shoulder. 'Thank you.'

102 A BABY TO HEAL THEIR HEARTS

'Actually, there is something else,' Bailey said. 'Obviously I wouldn't dream of breaking patient confidentiality, but I happen to know someone who had an ACL injury at your age, and I asked him for some advice for someone in your position.'

'Was he a tennis player?' Vivienne asked, looking interested.

'No, he was in a different sport,' Bailey said, 'but the injury and the rehab are the same. Actually, he offered to come and have a chat with you. He's waiting outside, if you'd like a word.'

Vivienne turned to her father, who nodded. 'That'd be great. Thanks.'

Bailey opened her office door and looked out; Jared glanced up, caught her eye and came to the door. 'She'd like to talk to me?' he asked.

'Yes. And thank you. I owe you,' she said.

'No. I'm just paying it forward,' he reminded her. 'Just as your patient will pay it forward, one day.'

It was a nice way of looking at it, Bailey

thought. She brought him into the room and introduced him to Vivienne and Mr Kaine.

'Well, I never. Jared Fraser—the England footballer. I remember watching you play years ago. You were amazing.' Mr Kaine shook Jared's hand. 'It's very good of you to come in and talk to us.'

'My pleasure,' Jared said.

'So do you still play for England?' Vivienne asked.

'No. Unfortunately, they couldn't fix my knee. Though that's *not* likely to be the case for you,' he emphasised, 'because Dr Randall tells me that you're a really good candidate for surgery. If you follow the rehab programme to the letter you'll be fine. Dr Randall asked me for my advice, and I thought it might be better for you to have it in person, just in case you have any questions.'

Vivienne nodded. 'Thank you very much, Mr Fraser.'

'Right now,' he said gently, 'it probably feels like the end of the world and you're worrying that you're going to lose so much ground against everyone else.'

She bit her lip. 'That's exactly how it feels.'

'So you need to take it one day at a time, and find someone you can talk to—someone who won't let you pity yourself, but will make you be sensible and get the right balance between doing enough work to strengthen your knee, but not so much that you damage it again and end up back at square one,' Jared said.

'That's good advice,' Mr Kaine agreed. 'I'll always listen, Vivi, but he's right—you do need someone else to talk to.'

'I was lucky,' Jared said. 'I had a great coach. And he made me see that although my knee wouldn't hold up enough for me to play at international level again, I had other options. I could learn to coach, or I could do what I ended up doing—I trained as a doctor, and I'm still part of the sport because nowadays I work with the youth team of a premiership division club. So even if there are complications in the future and you don't end up playing at this level again, you'll still have options—you can still be part of tennis.'

'I don't mean to be rude,' Vivienne said, 'but I don't want to be a coach or a doctor. I just want to play tennis. It's all I've ever wanted to do.'

'And you will play again,' Bailey said. 'But, as Dr Fraser said, you need to follow your rehab programme.'

'Waiting is the worst bit,' Jared said. 'You'll want to push yourself too hard. But don't. Use that time to study instead. Look at different techniques, look at the way your opponents play and use that to hone your strategy. To really succeed at a top level in sport you need just as much up here…' he tapped his head '…as you need the physical skills.'

'Vivi picked up a racket practically as soon as she could walk,' Mr Kaine said. 'I used to play—nothing like at her level—just at a club on Sunday afternoons, and her mum would bring her to watch. And she ended up joining in.' He ruffled her hair. 'When she started beating us hollow and she wasn't even ten years old, we knew we were seeing something special in the making. And you'll get that back, love. We just have to make sure we do everything the doctors tell us, OK?'

'OK,' Vivienne said.

Bailey smiled at them both. 'And I'll do my very best to help you get that knee back to how it was, so you can go and get those grand slams.'

'Can I be rude and ask, Mr Fraser, do you miss playing?' Vivienne asked.

'Sometimes,' Jared said. 'But I'm thirty-five now, so I'd be near the end of my professional playing career in any case. And I'm lucky because I really enjoy my job. It means I get the chance to help players fulfil their potential. If someone had told me that when I was your age, I would have laughed at them—but I really do feel I've achieved something when I see them grow and improve. So don't rule it out as something you might do when you're ready to retire from playing.'

Vivienne looked thoughtful, and Bailey could see that Jared's words had given her a different perspective—something that would make all the waiting during her rehab a lot easier. 'Thank you, Mr F—*Dr* Fraser,' she amended.

When the Kaines had left, Jared was about to follow them out when Bailey stopped him. 'Thanks for doing that, Jared—you've made a real difference to her.'

'No worries.'

'If I wasn't up to my eyes in paperwork and appointments,' she said, 'I'd offer to take you for lunch to thank you properly. Or dinner—but I'm doing bridesmaid stuff for Joni tonight. So please consider this a kind of rain check.' She took a plain white patisserie box from her desk drawer and handed it to him.

'What's this?' he asked.

She smiled. 'A little slice of heaven. Don't open it now. Tell me what you think later.'

'OK.' He looked intrigued. 'I'll text you. Good luck for tonight.'

'Thanks.'

Later that evening, she had a text that made her laugh.

Best chocolate cake in the universe. Would very much like to help with more patients. Quite happy to be paid in cake.

I'll see what I can do, she texted back.

Funny, when she'd first met Jared, she'd thought him grumpy and surly and a pain in the neck. Now she rather liked his dry sense of humour and the quiet, sensible way he went about things.

But she'd better not let herself get too close. After the way her marriage to Ed had splintered, she just didn't trust herself to get it right next time. It was best to stick to being colleagues. Friends, too, maybe; but she'd have to dampen down the attraction that sparkled through her veins every time she saw him. To keep her heart safe.

CHAPTER SIX

'Joni, you look beautiful,' Bailey said, surveying her best friend.

'So do you.' But Joni also looked worried. 'Bailey, are you sure you're OK?'

'Of course I am—why wouldn't I be?'

'Because I remember the last time that one of us was in a bridesmaid's dress and the other was the bride,' Joni said softly.

Bailey's wedding day. A day so full of promise. A day when she'd thought she couldn't be happier… And then, two short years later, she'd discovered that she couldn't be any more unhappy when her whole world crashed down around her. 'I'm fine. More than fine. Don't give it another moment's thought,' she said brightly. Even if she hadn't been fine, no way would Bailey rain on her best friend's parade on her wedding day.

'I can't believe you're actually bringing Herod as your plus-one.'

Bailey groaned. 'Please don't call him that when you meet him—he'll be mortified.'

'You've been very cagey about him. So you're getting on OK together now?'

'We've reached an understanding.'

Joni raised an eyebrow. '*That* sort of understanding?'

'Absolutely not. Even if I was looking for someone, Jared Fraser wouldn't make my list of potentials.' That was a big fat lie—Jared Fraser was one of the most attractive men she'd met, particularly when he smiled—but hopefully Joni would be too distracted by all the bridal stuff going on to call her on it. Bailey hoped. 'No, he's just doing me a favour and taking a bit of heat off me where my family's concerned.'

'As long as you're OK.'

'Of course I'm OK,' Bailey reassured her. 'I'm thrilled that my best friend's getting married to the love of her life, and I get to follow

her down the aisle in the most gorgeous bridesmaid's dress ever. Now, the car's going to be
here at any second, so we need to get moving.'

Jared took a deep breath and walked down the
path to the church. He hadn't been to a wedding
since his own marriage to Sasha. And, despite
Bailey's assurances that the bride and groom
were right for each other, Jared still felt awkward. A cynic who'd lost his belief in marriage
really shouldn't be here to celebrate a wedding.
He half wished Bailey was going to be there
with him to take his mind off it, but as she was
Joni's bridesmaid he knew that she would be the
very last person walking into the church, and
she wouldn't be sitting with him, either.

He really should have asked if he could at
least meet the bride and groom before the wedding, so he would know someone there. Right
at that moment he was really regretting the impulse that had made him offer to be Bailey's
'plus-one'.

His only consolation had been the text she'd

sent him that morning: See you at the church. And thank you. I appreciate it.

And being appreciated was nice. It had been a while since he'd last felt appreciated.

The usher greeted him with a smile. 'Bride's side or groom's?'

'Bride's,' Jared said, feeling a total fake.

'Sit anywhere on the left except the front two pews,' the usher said with a smile, handing him an order of service booklet.

Jared remembered the drill: anywhere except the front two pews, where the bride's and groom's immediate family would be sitting.

Over the next few minutes the church filled up. Two men walked down to the front of the church; one of them was obviously the groom and the other the best man, Jared thought.

A wedding.

A room full of hope, with everyone wishing the bride and groom happiness until the end of their days. But how often did that hope turn sour? How many people did he know who'd actually stayed together, apart from his parents and two of his siblings? Not that many.

The organist started to play the wedding march, and the bride walked in on her father's arm, looking gorgeous and deliriously happy. Behind her, carrying the long train and a bouquet of deep red roses—to match her knee-length dress and incredibly high-heeled shoes—was Bailey.

Jared had never seen her wearing make-up before, not even on that morning when they'd trained together and she'd come to breakfast in a suit. It was barely there—mainly mascara and a hint of lipstick, from what he could tell—but it served to show him that she was jaw-droppingly beautiful and didn't need anything to enhance her looks. Right now, she looked incredibly glamorous, a million miles away from the slightly scruffy doctor he was used to—the one who walked around the football pitch in tracksuit pants and a hoodie.

He caught her eye as she walked by and she actually winked at him.

And all the blood in his body rushed south.

Oh, help. They hadn't set any ground rules, so this might just be one of his biggest mistakes ever. God. He really should've agreed it with her beforehand. At the very least they should've agreed on no touching and no holding hands. And yet he was supposed to be her fake boyfriend. Everyone would expect him to hold her hand, put his arm round her, gaze at her adoringly, maybe even kiss her...

The idea of kissing her sent him into such a flat spin that he was barely aware of the marriage ceremony. But then the registers were signed and the bride and groom walked down the aisle, all smiles.

The usher handed him a box of bird-friendly confetti on the way out. Jared lined up on the side of the path to the church with everyone else and waited until the photographer directed them all to throw confetti over the happy couple.

He took a couple of photos on his phone and managed to catch one of Bailey with her head tipped back, laughing. The kind of picture that would make a rainy morning feel full of sunshine.

She came over to him while the bride and groom were being photographed on their own. 'Hey. Thanks for coming.'

'Pleasure.' And, actually, it was now. 'You, um, look very nice.'

'Thank you. So do you. I've never seen you in a proper suit before.' She grinned. 'I would say a suit "suits" you, but I need to find a better way of saying it.'

Funny, her easy manner put him at his ease, too. It suddenly didn't matter that this was a wedding, and all the darkness associated with the end of his own marriage just faded away—because Bailey was there and she *sparkled*.

'I'll introduce you properly to everyone at the reception,' she promised. 'Sorry, I should have organised this a lot better so I was travelling with you or something.'

'It's fine. You're the bridesmaid and you have things to do. I'll see you at the reception.'

She gave him another of those incredibly sexy winks. *'Ciao, bello.'*

The Italian side of her was really coming out today. He'd never really seen this before; but then again she'd never flirted with him before, either.

Oddly, he found himself looking forward to the reception—and what he really wanted to do was dance with her. Which was crazy, because he didn't even like dancing very much; but he had a feeling that Bailey did and that she'd be good at it.

He made his way to the hotel where the reception was being held, and joined the line-up of people waiting to kiss the bride and shake the groom's hand. Bailey came and found him in the line. 'Hey, there.'

'Hey.' How ridiculous was it that he should feel suddenly intimidated?

But Bailey took charge, making small talk until she could introduce him to the bride and groom. 'Jared, this is Joni and Aaron. Joni and Aaron, this is Jared Fraser.'

'Very pleased to meet you, Jared,' Joni said with a smile. Jared caught the meaningful look she gave Bailey, and wondered just what Bailey had told her best friend about him. 'Thanks for coming.'

'Thanks for inviting me. It was a lovely service, and you look gorgeous,' he said.

She kissed his cheek. 'You're too sweet. I knew Bailey was lying when she said you were grumpy.'

He laughed. 'I can be.' He gave Bailey a pointed look. 'Though so can she.'

'No way—she's the endorphin queen,' Joni said. 'Bailey believes endorphins are the answer to absolutely everything.'

Jared went hot all over, thinking just how endorphins could be released and how much he'd like to do that with her. He really hoped nobody could read his thoughts. But he managed to pull himself together and shook Aaron's hand. 'Congratulations, both of you, and I hope you'll be very happy together.'

They exchanged a glance, and he could see

just how much they adored each other. So maybe Bailey was right and this would have a happy ending. Maybe he should start to believe in love again.

'Righty.' Bailey tucked her arm into his. 'Let's get this over with. Come and meet my lot. They're the nicest family in the world, but I'm going to apologise in advance because they're a bit—well—full on.'

'Italian,' he said.

She nodded. 'Even though Dad's English, living with my mum and the rest of us has kind of made him Italian.'

'That's nice,' Jared said, and let her lead him over to her family.

'Jared, this is my mother, Lucia, my brothers, Roberto and Giorgio—Rob and Gio for short—and my dad, Paul.'

Jared shook hands and kissed cheeks as expected, and then turned to Bailey. 'How come you don't have an Italian first name?' he asked.

'Because I was born on Christmas Eve, and in my family it's tradition to watch *It's a Wonder-*

ful Life every single Christmas Eve—including the year I was born, because Mum had me at home. So she really had to call me Bailey, after George's family.'

'It could be worse,' Lucia said with a grin. 'I could have called you Clarence.'

'Clarrie. Yes. That's *so* me.' Bailey flapped her hands in imitation of an angel's wings and laughed.

'She's kept you very quiet, Jared,' Lucia said.

'Because we haven't known each other very long, and I know what you're like, Mamma,' Bailey said. She switched into rapid Italian; clearly she was asking her mother not to interrogate him or embarrass her, Jared thought. Mischief prompted him to ask her if she realised that he spoke Italian, just to tease her; but, knowing Bailey, she'd call his bluff and speak in Italian for the rest of the evening, so he resisted the temptation. Just.

'Sì, sì, bambina mia.' Lucia pinched Bailey's cheeks, and then continued her interrogation. 'So where did you meet, Jared?'

'At work,' he said carefully.

'So you're a doctor?'

'For a football team, yes.'

Bailey's dad smiled at him. 'Which one?'

Jared named the premier division club. 'I work with the youth team—and they've got real potential.'

'Oh, the team Bailey's testing her box of tricks on?' Paul asked. 'I thought you said the team doctor was about to retire, Bailey?'

'He did. Jared took over from him,' Bailey said. 'Are you going to grill the poor man all night, or can we talk about something else— like how gorgeous my best friend looks in her lovely floaty dress?'

'She does indeed.' Paul gave her a hug. 'And so do you, darling. We don't see you dressed up like this very often.'

'If you came to see me with a sports injury and I looked like this when I treated you, you'd be worried that I didn't have a clue what I was talking about and think that you were going to be injured and in pain for the rest of your life,' she said with a grin. 'That's why I don't dress like this very often.'

It turned out that they were at a table with Bailey's family for the wedding breakfast, and Jared was surprised by how easily they included him in the conversation, as if they'd known him for ever. In turn, he got them to talk about the restaurant—and learned a lot about Bailey as a child. Her family was merciless in telling tales; but they clearly adored her, because she was laughing along with the rest of them and giving just as good as she got by telling tales about them, too.

He discovered that Bailey, when she was with her family, was incredibly tactile, so it was just as well they hadn't agreed a no-touching rule, because she would've broken it several times a minute. He already knew that she talked with her hands, but this was something else. She touched his arm, his shoulder, his face, his hair. He wasn't used to that at all, but he was surprised to discover that he liked it. That he wanted more.

Though that wasn't part of the deal. He was her fake partner for tonight, not her real one, he reminded himself.

The food was excellent, but best of all was the cake. 'This has to be the best cake I've ever had in my life,' he said.

Rob looked pleased. 'I'm glad you like it. Actually, it's one of mine,' he said diffidently.

'Bailey said you were good—but she didn't say you were *this* good. And I'm going to beg for seconds.'

'You weren't listening properly,' she said, cuffing his arm. 'I told you Rob was the best pastry chef in the universe. And who do you think made that chocolate cake I gave you?'

'Oh, now, with those two pieces of evidence, I agree completely,' Jared said with a smile.

Funny, he'd been faintly dreading the reception. But it was all easy, from chatting at the tables to listening to the speeches. And then finally the band started playing and the dancing began. The bride and groom danced together first, followed by Bailey and the best man. Jared couldn't take his eyes off her. The way she moved was so graceful, so elegant. This was yet another side to the clever, slightly acerbic doctor he was used to. She'd turned out to be full of surprises.

And then she came over to him. 'Dance with me?'

How could he say no? Especially when he'd been wanting to hold her close all day, and this was the perfect excuse.

When he danced with her, it was the first time he'd ever noticed her perfume; it reminded him of an orange grove in full bloom, yet with a sweet undertone. Sparkly and warm, just like her personality. And he could feel the warmth of her body against his.

To keep his mind off that fact, he asked, 'Why do I recognise the guy playing guitar with the band?'

'That's Olly, Joni's brother—he was one of the ushers, so you would've met him at the church,' she explained.

'Oh.'

'Sorry about my family earlier. As I said, they're a little intense.'

'Don't apologise—I like them. They love you,' he said, 'and it's pretty clear they worry about you.'

She rolled her eyes. 'I'm thirty years old. I can look after myself.'

'Families are supposed to worry about you,' he reminded her.

'Does yours worry about you?' she challenged.

He smiled. 'When I let them, yes.'

'So you're as bad as I am—except I bet you keep yours at bay by being grumpy.'

'And you keep yours at bay by sparkling,' he fenced.

'Sparkling?'

'Like vintage champagne in candlelight,' he said.

Oh, for goodness' sake. Anyone would think he'd been drinking way too much of the vintage champagne. He simply didn't wax poetic like that. But something about Bailey made the words flow and he couldn't stop them.

She smiled. 'You think I'm sparkly?'

'Very,' he admitted.

'Thank you—that's a really lovely thing to say. Especially as I've pretty much neglected you today, and you're doing me a huge favour by being here in the first place.'

'You haven't neglected me.' And he was suddenly really glad that he'd agreed to do this. Because he was seeing a new side to Bailey Randall—a side he really liked. Sweet and playful and totally charming; yet it was totally genuine.

He held her closer. Somehow they were dancing cheek to cheek, and his hand was splayed at the top of her dress. He could feel the warmth of her skin against his fingertips and it sent a thrill right through him. Right at that moment it felt as if it was just the two of them on the dance floor, with nobody else around for miles and miles and miles.

'Your back is perfect,' he murmured.

'Why, thank you, Dr Fraser.'

'Sorry.' He sighed. 'I didn't mean to say that. Ignore me.'

She pulled back slightly to look him straight in the eye. 'I wasn't being sarcastic—and I wasn't offended. Seriously, Jared, thank you for the compliment.'

Her mouth was beautiful; her lower lip was full and he itched to catch it between his.

Oh, this was bad.

Why was he thinking about kissing her?

'I noticed how perfect your back was when we trained together,' he said. And now he was making things much worse. He really needed to shut up.

She ran one finger down his sleeve. 'And I noticed your biceps when we trained together.' Her voice had grown husky. 'I like your biceps. They're perfect, too.'

He knew that he was supposed to be just playing the part of her partner, but right now he wanted to make it reality. So he dipped his head. Just a little bit. Just enough that his mouth could brush against hers.

She tasted of champagne and wedding cake—and he liked it. A lot.

He pulled back so he could look her in the eye and take his cue from her. If she wanted him to back off, he'd do it.

But her lips were ever so slightly parted and there was a sparkle in her eyes that he'd never seen before.

'Bailey, I really want to kiss you,' he whispered.

'I want you to kiss me, too,' she whispered back.

That was all the encouragement he needed. He dipped his head again and took his sweet time kissing her. Every brush of his mouth against hers, every nibble, made him more and more aware of her. And she was kissing him back, her arms wrapped as tightly round him as his were round her.

He wanted this to last for ever.

But then he became aware that the music had changed and become more uptempo, and he and Bailey were still swaying together as if the band was playing a slow song. He broke the kiss, and he could see the exact moment that she realised what was going on, too. Those gorgeous dark eyes were absolutely huge. And she looked as shocked as he felt. Panicked, almost.

This wasn't supposed to be happening.

'I, um…' she said, and tailed off.

'Yeah.' He didn't know what to say, either. What he really wanted to do was kiss her again—but they were in a public place. With her best friend and her family in attendance. And doing what he really wanted to do would cause all kinds of complications. He didn't want to get involved with anyone. Apart from that one awful evening when his best friend had persuaded him to try speed dating—an experience he never wanted to repeat—Jared hadn't dated since his divorce. No way was he setting himself up to get hurt again, the way he he'd been with Sasha—even though he knew that Bailey wasn't a bit like Sasha.

'I guess I ought to do some chief bridesmaid stuff and get the kids dancing,' she said.

And he ought to offer to help her. Except there was just a hint of fear in her eyes. He didn't think she was scared of him; maybe, he thought, she was just as scared of getting involved as he was. Especially given that she'd asked him to be her fake partner to keep her family happy. Bailey had obviously been hurt at some point, too, and they clearly worried about her.

'I guess,' he said. 'Do you, um, want a hand?'

'Do you like kids?'

That was an easy one. 'Yes, I do.' And he'd always thought he'd have children of his own one day. Sasha had taken the choice of keeping the baby away from him, and at that point he'd realised just how much he wanted to be a dad. But unless he took the risk of giving someone his heart—the right woman, someone he could really trust—that wasn't going to happen.

He pushed the thought away and concentrated on helping Bailey organise the children. She was a natural with them—they responded to her warmth. Just like him.

'If you could dance with some of the wallflowers,' she said quietly to him, 'that would be kind.'

Kind wasn't what he was feeling right now, but kind would be a hell of a lot safer. 'Sure,' he said.

Even though he was polite and made conversation with the women he danced with, he was totally aware of Bailey throughout the entire evening. Her smile, her sparkle, her warmth. And she made him ache.

He wanted her. Really wanted her. But he knew she'd panicked as much as he had when they'd kissed, so it was a bad idea. They needed to go back to being strictly colleagues. Somehow.

At the end of the evening he said his goodbyes to Bailey's family, trusting that she'd manage to get him out of a promise to see them soon.

'I guess this is it, then,' she said as she walked him to the door of the ballroom.

'I'll call a taxi and see you home first,' he said.

She shook her head. 'You don't have to do that.'

He smiled. 'Yes, I do. I'm old-fashioned. So let's not argue about it—just humour me on this one, OK?'

She didn't argue and let him organise a taxi. She didn't say much on the journey back to her place; although Jared desperately wanted to reach for her hand, he kept a tight rein on himself and simply joined her in sitting quietly.

When the taxi stopped, he paid the cabbie.

'Isn't he taking you home now?' Bailey asked, and he could see the panic in her eyes. Did she really think that he expected her to invite him in for a nightcap—or more?

'No. I'm seeing you to your doorstep and waiting until you're safely inside, then I'm taking the Tube home,' Jared said. 'And, yes, I know you can look after yourself, but it's been a long day and you're wearing incredibly high heels.'

'Point taken.' Her expression softened. 'Thank you.'

She let him escort her to her doorstep.

'Thank you for today,' she said. 'I really appreciate it.'

'No worries.' He leaned forward, intending to give her a reassuring—and strictly platonic— kiss on the cheek. But somewhere along the way one or both of them moved their head, and the next thing he knew his lips were skimming against hers.

What started out as a soft, sweet, gentle kiss quickly turned to something else entirely, and he was kissing her as if he was starving. She was kissing him right back, opening her mouth to let him deepen the kiss. And this felt so right, so perfect.

When she pulled away, his head was swimming.

'No,' she said. 'We can't do this.'

The panic was back in her face.

Her ex, whoever he was, must have really hurt her badly, Jared thought.

And he had no intention of making her feel worse.

'It's OK.' He took her hand and squeezed it. Just once. The way she'd squeezed his hand when he'd talked about his knee injury. Sympathy, not pity. 'You're right. We're colleagues, and *just* colleagues.'

And he needed to keep that in mind. He didn't want the complication of falling for someone, either. The risk of everything going wrong. Been there, done that and learned from his mistakes.

The fear in her eyes faded—just a fraction, but she'd clearly heard what he'd said.

'I'll see you at work,' he said.

'Yeah. I'll see you.' She swallowed. 'And I'm sorry.'

'There's nothing to be sorry for,' he said.

He waited until she'd unlocked her front door and closed it again behind her, and then he left to find the Tube station. It was better this way. Being sensible.

Wasn't it?

CHAPTER SEVEN

BAILEY SLEPT REALLY badly that night. Every
time she closed her eyes, all she could see was
Jared in that wretched suit, looking totally
edible. Worse, her mouth tingled in memory of
the way he'd kissed her.

OK, she'd admit it. She was attracted to Jared
Fraser. Big time.

But, after the way her marriage had imploded,
she wasn't sure she could risk getting involved
with anyone again. Letting herself be vulnerable. Risking the same thing happening all
over again. After the ectopic pregnancy she'd
ended up pushing Ed away—physically as well
as emotionally—because she'd been so scared
of getting pregnant again.

So, as much as she would like to date Jared—
and to take things a lot further than they had at
the wedding—she was going to be sensible and

keep things between them just as colleagues. Because she didn't want to hurt him, the way she'd hurt Ed.

Do you like kids?

And he'd said yes. She could imagine him as a father, especially after she'd seen him with the children at the wedding. And that was another sticking point. She wanted children, too. But the ectopic pregnancy had shredded her confidence. What if it happened again and her other tube ruptured, leaving her infertile?

She'd been terrified of getting pregnant again, and that had made her scared of sex—a vicious circle she hadn't been able to break. Technically, Ed had been unfaithful to her; but Bailey blamed herself for it, because he'd only done it after she'd pushed him away and refused to let him touch her. She knew that the break-up of her marriage was all her fault.

Since her divorce, until Jared, she hadn't met anyone she'd wanted to date. But how could she expect him to deal with all her baggage? It wouldn't be fair.

So, the next morning, she sent Jared a text to clear the air—and also to make it very clear to him how she felt. And hopefully it would ease any potential awkwardness at work.

Sorry. Too much champagne yesterday. Hope I haven't wrecked our professional relationship.

Jared read the message for the fourth time.

Too much champagne? Hardly. He'd been watching Bailey. She'd had one glass, maybe two. With a meal. Most of the time she'd been drinking sparkling water—as had he.

It was an excuse, and he knew it. She'd looked so scared. As panicky as he'd felt. But why?

Next time he saw her, he decided, he'd get her to talk to him. For now, he'd try to keep things easy between them.

Medicinal recommendation of a fry-up for the hangover, he texted back. See you on the pitch later in the week.

Facing Jared for the first time since the wedding made Bailey squirm inside. In the end, she decided to brazen it out. Hadn't he said she was sparkly? Then she'd go into super-sparkly mode. So she chatted to all the players, gave Archie a smacking kiss hello on the cheek—while making quite sure she was out of grabbing reach half a second later—and gave Jared a lot of backchat about being too old and too stuck in his ways to do yoga with the boys in the team.

To her relief, he responded the same way, and things were back to the way they used to be. Before he'd kissed her.

Almost.

Because during the training session she looked up from her laptop and caught him looking at her; those amazing blue eyes were filled with wistfulness.

Yeah.

She'd like to repeat that kiss, too. Take things further. But she just couldn't take the risk. She knew he'd end up being just as hurt as she was. She couldn't destroy him, the way she'd destroyed Ed.

* * *

'Can we have a word?' Jared asked at the end of the training session.

'Um—sure.' Bailey looked spooked.

He waited until the players and Archie had gone into the dressing room. 'Are you OK?' he asked gently.

'Of course. Why wouldn't I be?'

'You and me. Saturday night,' he pointed out.

'Too much champagne,' she said swiftly.

'I don't think so.' He kept his voice soft. 'I think you're running scared.'

She lifted her chin and gave him a look that was clearly supposed to be haughty, but instead he saw the vulnerability there. 'I'm not scared.'

'That,' he said, 'is pure bravado. And I know that, because this thing between us scares me, too.'

The fight went out of her. 'Oh.'

'So what are we going to do about it?' he asked.

'I'm not looking for a relationship. I'm fine being single.'

'That's what I've been telling myself, too.' He paused. 'Maybe we could be brave. Together.'

'I…' She shook her head. 'I'm not ready for this.'

'Fair enough.' He held her gaze. 'But when you are…'

She swallowed hard. 'Yeah. I, um, ought to let you get on.'

He let her go. For now. And he could be patient, because Bailey Randall was definitely worth waiting for.

Everything was fine for the next week, until Bailey's system picked up a marked problem. Maybe it was a glitch in the system, she thought, and decided to keep it to herself for the time being. But when the same result showed after the next session, and after she'd caught the tail end of the lads gossiping outside the dressing room, she knew that she was going to have to do something.

'Jared, can we have a quick word?' she asked quietly.

He frowned. 'Is something wrong?'

'I think so.' She gestured to her laptop, so he'd know that it was to do with the monitoring system and one of the players.

'Hadn't we better talk to Archie if you want to pull someone from the team?' he asked.

She shook her head and kept her voice low. 'This is a tricky one, and you're the only person I can talk to about it.'

'OK,' he said. 'I assume you mean somewhere quiet, away from the club.'

'Definitely away from the club,' she said. 'Yes, please.'

'Are you free straight after training?'

She nodded.

'We'll talk then.'

'Thank you.' And just knowing that she could share this with him and he'd help her work out what to do made some of the sick feeling go away.

After the session, Jared took Bailey to a café not far from the football club. 'Sit down, and I'll get us some coffee.' He remembered what she'd drunk at the gym. 'I take it you'd like a latte?'

She smiled. 'I'm half-Italian. You only drink lattes at breakfast. Espresso for me, please.'

He smiled back. 'Sure.'

'And can I be greedy and ask for some cake, too?' she asked. 'I don't care what sort, as long as it's cake.'

'It's not going to be up to your brother's standards,' he warned.

'Right now, I don't care—I need the sugar rush.'

Worry flickered down Jared's spine. Whatever she wanted to discuss with him was clearly something serious if she needed a sugar rush. And he'd noticed that she'd been much quieter than normal during the training session.

He came back with two coffees, a blueberry muffin and a double chocolate muffin. 'You can have first pick.'

'Thank you.' She took the blueberry one.

He sat down opposite her. 'Spit it out. What's worrying you?'

'You know how my system picks up if someone's underperforming?'

'Yes.'

'I'm worried about one of the players. I've heard the rumours that he's in danger of losing his place on the team because he hasn't been playing well for a while.'

'Darren,' Jared said immediately.

She nodded. 'And I heard the boys talking. He's not coping with the pressure.' She sighed. 'It's hearsay and I don't want to accuse him of something when he might be perfectly innocent, but...' Her eyes were huge with concern. 'I think he's drinking. Apart from it making his performance worse, he's not even eighteen yet—he's underage.'

Jared blew out a breath. 'I've known a few players over the years who started drinking to handle the pressure, and it finished their careers.'

She looked miserable. 'I don't know what to do. If I tell Archie, then Darren will definitely lose his place. He'll be kicked out.'

'For breaking his contract,' Jared agreed.

'But if he *is* drinking, then it needs to stop right now, Jared. He's going to damage himself.'

'Agreed.'

'Maybe I'm being a bit paranoid and over-thinking it. Have a look and see what you reckon.' She opened her laptop and drew up the graphs. Darren's performance had been very near his average in every session apart from the last two, where there was a marked difference.

'So you suspected it last time as well?' he asked.

She nodded. 'I wanted to monitor a second performance, just in case the first one was a one-off—a glitch in the programme or some-thing.'

'No, I think your analysis is spot on. We need to tell Archie and Lyle Fincham.'

'But they'll kick him out.'

'Not necessarily. We can both put in a good word for him. He's not a bad kid—he's just made a mistake and he needs some help.' Jared shrugged. 'Extra coaching might make things easier for him, and I can design a workout programme tailored to his needs.'

'You'd do that for him?' She sounded surprised.

'Everyone makes mistakes. And everyone deserves a second chance,' he said. 'A chance to put it right.'

He hoped she'd think about it. And that she'd give them a second chance, too.

Mr Fincham wasn't available, so Jared and Bailey tackled Archie.

'So there's a problem with one of the players?' Archie asked.

Bailey nodded and talked the team coach through the computer evidence.

Archie frowned. 'So you think he's drinking?'

'You know as well as I do, some players do when they can't cope with the pressure,' Jared said.

'And it only makes things worse. Plus he's underage. If he can't cope, then he'll have to leave the team,' Archie said with a sigh. 'I can't have him being a bad influence on the rest of the lads.'

'Or,' Bailey said, 'you could give him another chance. We could talk to him and tell him what damage he's doing to himself—in graphic enough terms to make him stop.'

'And I can give him an extra training programme to help him brush up his skills and make him feel that some of the pressure's off,' Jared said.

'If the papers get hold of this, the muck will really hit the fan,' Archie said, and shook his head. 'No. He'll have to go.'

'Archie. It's happened *twice*. That's not so bad—he'll be able to stop. Give the boy a chance to come good,' Bailey urged.

'And what message does that give the others? That I'm soft on the kind of behaviour that destroys a team?'

'No. It tells them that you understand they're still very young and some of them need a bit more guidance than others,' Jared said.

'Lyle won't be happy about it,' Archie warned.

'But you can talk him round. You're the team coach. He'll listen to you,' Bailey said.

Archie didn't look totally convinced. 'And what if Darren does it again?'

'Then there are all kinds of disciplinary options,' Jared said.

'But if we all give him the right support,' Bailey added, 'he won't do it again.'

Archie went silent, clearly thinking about it. 'All right,' he said. 'I'll square it with Lyle. But I'm going to read young Darren the Riot Act and make sure he knows that if he puts a single toe out of line from now on, he'll be out.'

'Thank you,' Bailey said.

'Everyone deserves a second chance,' Jared added. 'I think he'll make the most of it.'

Everyone deserves a second chance.

Could that be true for them, too? Bailey wondered.

Jared had clearly been thinking about it, too, because later that evening he called her. 'Are you busy?'

'I'm studying,' she said.

'Have you eaten yet?'

'Yes.' A sandwich at her desk. But it counted.

'Oh.' He paused. 'I wondered if you'd like to have dinner with me.'

Was he asking her on a date? Adrenalin fizzed through her veins. Strange how Jared made her feel like a teenager. 'As colleagues?' she asked carefully.

'No.'

So he *did* mean a date. Excitement was replaced by skittering panic. 'I'll think about it.'

'Is my company really that bad?' he asked.

'No—no, it's not that, Jared. Not at all.' She sighed. 'It's complicated.'

'I can take a hint.'

She *would* like to have dinner with him; it was just that the whole idea of dating again scared her. How could she tell him, without dumping all that baggage on him? Telling him what had happened to her, and why her marriage had ended? She couldn't. She just couldn't. 'I, um, haven't dated in a while,' she said.

'Me, neither,' he said, surprising her. 'I'm seriously out of practice, too.'

Something else they had in common. Who, she wondered, had hurt him?

'I was thinking,' he said, 'we were a good team, this afternoon.'

'Yes.'

'And I was thinking,' he said, 'maybe we should give ourselves a chance to see if we could be a good team outside work.'

'Maybe,' she said.

'I could,' he suggested, 'cook dinner for you.'

'You can cook?'

He coughed. 'Don't be sexist. Especially as your brothers are both chefs.'

She smiled wryly. 'Yeah, I guess.'

'So—how about it?'

'If I say yes,' she said, 'then it's just between us?'

'You want to keep it a secret?' He sounded slightly hurt.

'I want to keep life simple,' she said. 'Can I think about it?'

'It's just as well I'm a sports doctor. My ego could really use some liniment right now,' he said dryly.

And now he'd made her laugh. He was the first man to do that in a long while. Maybe, just maybe, she should give this a try. Maybe everyone was right and it was time she learned to live again. And Jared might just be the man to help her do that.

'All right. Thank you, Jared. I'd like to have dinner with you. I don't have any food allergies and I'm not fussy about what I eat.'

'That was a quick decision.'

And she still wasn't sure it was the right one. Part of her really, really wanted to do it; and part of her wanted to run. 'When do you want to do it?' Oh, and that sounded bad. She felt her face heat. Worse still, that was a definite Freudian slip. Because any woman with red blood in her veins would want to go to bed with someone as sexy as Jared Fraser. 'Have dinner, I mean,' she added hastily.

'Tomorrow night?' he suggested.

'That's fine.' Big, fat lie. Now they'd actually set a date, the panic was back. In triplicate. 'I'll need your address.'

'Got a pen?'

'Give me two seconds.' She grabbed a pen. 'OK, tell me.' She scribbled down his address as he dictated it. 'What time?'

'Seven?'

'Seven,' she confirmed. 'Can I bring anything? Pudding, maybe?' She could get Rob to make something special. Then again, Rob would tell their mother, and Lucia would go straight into interrogation mode. OK. She'd cheat and buy it from a top-end supermarket instead.

'No, that's fine. Just bring yourself,' he said.

And how scary that sounded.

Bailey was feeling antsy the next morning, and she was really glad that she was busy all day in clinic. There were the usual sprains and strains, although she did feel a bit sorry for the middle-aged woman who'd managed to give herself tennis elbow from taking her weightlifting training too hard and was horrified to learn it could take several months of rest before the tear in her ligament healed.

'Rest, ice it every couple of hours, take painkillers and use a support bandage when you exercise and whenever it's really sore,' Bailey said. 'And when you do go back to using weights, you'll need to drop the weights right down and take it very steadily. And don't do anything above your head before it's healed fully, or your rotator cuff in your shoulder will overcompensate for your elbow and you'll have to get over the damage to that, too.'

Mrs Curtis grimaced. 'I knew I shouldn't have done that last set. I just wanted to finish the last few reps, but I should've just admitted that I was tired and stopped there.'

'You'll know next time,' Bailey said. 'Come back and see me if it's not any better within a couple of weeks. It should heal on its own, but if it doesn't then a corticosteroid injection could help.'

'Thank you.' Mrs Curtis smiled wryly. 'That'll teach me to remember how old I am, not how old I feel.'

Bailey patted her shoulder. 'We all do it. Don't beat yourself up about it.'

She bought wine and chocolates on the way home, and changed her outfit three times before deciding that smart casual was the way forward—a little black dress would be way too much. Black trousers and a silky long-sleeved teal top would be better. She added her nice jet earrings to give her courage, put on a slightly brighter shade of lipstick than she would normally and then stared at herself in the mirror.

How long had it been since she'd gone on a first date? Or since someone had cooked for her? How did you even behave in these sorts of situations? She thought about calling Joni and asking for help—but, then again, it would make Joni think she was really serious about Jared, and… No, it was all too complicated. She had no idea how he made her feel, other than that he put her in a flat spin.

'It's dinner. Just dinner,' she told her reflection. 'Treat him as a friend. A colleague. And then everything will be fine.'

Except she knew she was lying. Because since that kiss, she hadn't thought of Jared as a colleague—or as a friend. And he hadn't asked her to dinner as a colleague or friend, either.

Would he kiss her again tonight?

And she wasn't sure if the shiver down her spine was anticipation or fear.

CHAPTER EIGHT

BAILEY'S PANIC GREW as she walked up the path to Jared's door. She almost didn't ring the bell and scuttled home to safety instead, but she knew that would be unkind and unfair. He'd gone to the effort of cooking her a meal, so the least she could do was turn up to eat it—even if she did feel way more jumpy than the proverbial cat on a hot tin roof.

She took a deep breath and rang the bell.

When he answered the door, she was glad she'd opted for smart casual, because he'd done the same. He was wearing black trousers and a dark blue shirt that brought out the colour of his eyes. She could feel herself practically dissolving into a puddle of hormones, and her social skills had all suddenly deserted her.

How had she forgotten just how gorgeous the man was?

And his biceps.

Don't think about his biceps, she told herself. Concentrate. Friends and colleagues.

She handed him the wine and chocolates. 'I forgot to ask you if I should bring red or white, so I played it safe—and I should've asked you if you like milk, white or dark chocolate.' Oh, help. Now she was gabbling and she sounded like a fool.

'These are just fine, and you really didn't need to bring them—but I appreciate it,' he said.

And, oh, that smile was to die for. The butterflies in her tummy went into stampede mode.

'Come in.' He stood aside and gestured for her to enter.

How come he didn't look anywhere near as nervous as she felt? How could he be so cool and relaxed when she was a gibbering wreck?

She followed him inside, her tension and anticipation growing with every step.

'We're eating in the kitchen. I hope that's OK,' he said, obviously trying to put her at ease.

'That's very OK, thanks.' His kitchen was

gorgeous: a deep terracotta tiled floor teamed with glossy cream cabinets, dark worktops and duck-egg-blue walls. There was a small square maple table at one end with two places set. 'I really like the way you've done your kitchen,' she said.

'I'm afraid it's all my sister's idea rather than mine,' he confessed. 'When I bought this place and did it up, she offered to paint for two hours a day until it was done if I would let her choose the kitchen.'

It sounded as if he was as close to his family as she was to hers. 'So you're not really a cook, then?'

'Given that you come from a family of restaurateurs and chefs, I wouldn't dare claim to be a cook,' he said.

She smiled. 'I promise I won't go into food critic mode.'

He pretended to mop his brow in relief, making her smile. 'Can I get you a drink?'

'Yes, please—whatever you're having.'

He took a bottle of Pinot Grigio from the

fridge and poured them both a glass. Bailey noted that all his appliances were built-in and hidden behind doors to match the rest of the cabinets. Efficient and stylish at the same time. She liked that. It was how she organised her own kitchen.

'Have a seat,' he said, indicating the table.

'Thanks.' She bit her lip. 'Sorry. As I said, it's been a while since I dated.'

'Me, too. And it's hard to know what to say. We could make small talk about the team and work—but then it wouldn't be like a date.'

'And if we ask each other about ourselves, it'll feel like—well—we're grilling each other,' she said.

'Or speed dating.' He grimaced. 'I let my best friend talk me into that one six months ago. Never, *ever* again.'

Speed dating was something she'd never done—along with signing up to an online dating agency or letting anyone set her up on a blind date. She'd made it clear to everyone that she was just fine as she was. 'Was it really that bad?'

'Probably slightly worse,' he said. 'But how do you meet someone when you get to our age?'

'You make us sound middle-aged.' She laughed, even though she knew what he meant. By their age, most people had already settled into a relationship or had a lot of baggage that made starting a new relationship difficult. It wasn't like when you were just out of university and there were parties every weekend where most of the people there were still single.

'I'm thirty-five—and sometimes I feel really middle-aged,' he said wryly, 'especially when I hear the seventeen-year-olds talking in the changing room about their girlfriends.'

She raised an eyebrow. 'They don't do that in front of me. Probably because they think I'll tell them off.' Then she groaned, 'Which means they think I'm old enough to be their mother, and at thirty I'm not *quite* that old.'

'Or maybe they've got a secret crush on you

and don't want to sound stupid in front of you,' Jared suggested.

'I think,' she said, 'that might be a slightly worse thought. They're still practically babies!'

He laughed and raised his glass. 'To us,' he said, 'and finding some way to talk to each other.'

'To us,' she echoed, feeling ridiculously shy.

'I forgot to ask you if you like fish,' he said.

'I do.'

'Good. Though I'm afraid I cheated on the starter,' he admitted. 'Which is ready right now.'

He took two plates from the fridge: baby crabs served in their shell with a salad garnish, and served with thin slices of rye bread and proper butter.

'I don't care if you cheated. This is lovely,' she said.

The main course was sea bass baked in foil with slices of lemon, rosemary potatoes, fine green beans and baby carrots. 'This is fabulous,' she said. 'Super-healthy and super-scrumptious.'

He inclined his head in acknowledgement of the compliment. 'Thank you.'

Pudding was a rich dark chocolate mousse served in a tiny pot with raspberries.

'Now, this,' Bailey said after the first mouthful, 'is what you'd use to make any woman say yes.'

And then she realised what she'd said.

She put one hand to her face in horror. 'Please tell me I didn't say that out loud.'

'I'm afraid you did.' His voice had grown slightly husky, and his pupils were huge, making his eyes look dark.

She blew out a breath. 'Um. I don't know what to say.'

'If it helps, I didn't actually make it with the intention of using it to seduce you,' he said. 'Only...you've put an image in my head now.'

'An image?'

He nodded. 'Of me feeding you this, one spoonful at a time.'

So much for telling herself to treat this as just dinner with a friend. Right now, he'd put exactly the same image in her own head and she could hardly breathe. Especially as she could vividly remember what it had felt like when he'd kissed her.

What would happen if she held out her spoon to him? Would he let her feed the rich chocolate mousse to him? Or would he lean forward and kiss her?

Time hung, suspended.

Which of them would make the first move?

Dark colour was slashed across his cheekbones. And she could feel the heat in her own face. The beat of desire.

Would he kiss her again?

'I think,' he said, his voice even huskier now, 'we probably need coffee.'

And some distance between them so they could both calm down again. 'Yes,' she whispered.

Though she couldn't help watching him while he moved round the kitchen. For someone who was over six feet tall and so muscular, he was very light on his feet. He'd moved lightly when he'd danced with her, too. What would it be like if he…?

No.

Do not think of Jared Fraser naked, she told herself.

Except she couldn't get the idea out of her head.

What would it be like, making love with Jared?

Her face heating even more, she tried to push the thought to the back of her mind and concentrated on her pudding. He did likewise when he'd finished making them both an espresso.

Silence stretched between them like wires, tighter and tighter.

They needed to break the tension now. Right now. Before they did something stupid. Like kissing each other until they were both dizzy. Right at that moment it was what she really wanted him to do. And she didn't dare look at him in case he didn't feel the same—or, worse, in case he did. She wasn't sure which scared her more.

She sipped the coffee. 'This is good,' she murmured. Oh, for pity's sake. Where was her stock of small talk when she needed it? Why couldn't she talk to him about books and films and theatre?

Probably because her tastes were on the girly side and his would be decidedly masculine.

'I'm glad you like the coffee.' He paused. 'Would you like to sit in the living room?'

'Can I help you wash up first?'

'No. That's what a dishwasher is for,' he said.

Actually, it probably wouldn't be a good idea to work with him in the kitchen. It would be way too easy to brush against each other. Turn to each other. *Touch each other...*

She followed him into his living room. Everything was in neutral tones and comfortable. There were several framed photographs on the mantelpiece and she couldn't resist putting her coffee down so she could look at them more closely. His graduation, three more graduation photographs of what had to be his brothers and his sister as they looked so like him, wedding photographs of his brothers and sister, and various family portraits—including one of him with a small child.

His daughter? Or maybe she was his niece or his godchild. If he'd had a daughter, he would've mentioned it when they talked about kids at Joni's wedding, surely?

'Your family?' she asked.

'Yes. Also known as the doctors at Lavender Lane Surgery.' He smiled. 'They try to poach me onto the team every so often, but I like what I'm doing now.'

Then she came to a picture of a football team. Judging by the haircuts, she'd say the picture was nearly twenty years old. So it was pretty obvious what that represented. His first ever international match. But something had puzzled her for ages. 'So how come, given that you have a Scots accent and a Scots surname, you played for England?'

'I was born in London,' he said, 'and my mum's English—so technically I could have played for either team, but as I lived in London I guess it made more sense to play for England.'

He smiled. 'Dad said if my team ever played the under-twenty-one Scotland team, his loyalties would've been really divided.'

'Like in our house. Whenever England plays Italy in the World Cup the boys end up cheering both sides.'

She picked him out immediately in the middle of the photograph. Mainly because that was the one she'd seen when she'd snooped on the Internet—not that she was going to tell him that. 'That's you at seventeen?'

'Yes—the first time I played for England.' He smiled. 'It was an amazing feeling. And when I scored that goal, it felt like all my birthdays and Christmases at once.'

'I bet.' On impulse, she turned round and hugged him.

Big mistake, because then his arms came round her, and he dipped his head to kiss her. His mouth was warm and sweet and tempting, and she found herself responding, letting him deepen the kiss.

He picked her up and carried her over to the

sofa, still kissing her, then settled down with her on his lap.

Right at that moment she really wanted him to carry her to his bed. To take her clothes off, bit by bit, and kiss every inch of skin as he uncovered it. And then to touch her again, make her forget about everything in the universe except him…

But then reality rushed back in. She wasn't on the Pill. She hadn't needed to be, because she'd steered clear of relationships, let alone sex. Condoms weren't always effective. If they made love, what if she got pregnant, and what if…? She swallowed hard. She could still remember being rushed into the emergency department, the crippling pain in her abdomen followed by an even worse pain in her soul. And it froze her.

Jared was aware that Bailey had stopped kissing him back. He pulled away slightly and he saw she looked incredibly panicky. Something had clearly happened in her past, something that had put absolute devastation in her eyes.

He stroked her face. 'Bailey, it's all right. We can stop right now and I'm not going to push you.'

But the fear didn't seem to go away. She remained where she was, looking haunted.

'If you want to talk to me,' he said, 'I'll listen, and whatever you tell me won't go any further than me.'

'I don't want to talk about it,' she muttered.

'That's OK, too.' He kept holding her close. He had a few trust issues, too, thanks to Sasha cheating on him and then not giving him any say in keeping the baby. But he really liked what he'd seen of Bailey. It would be worth the effort of learning to trust and teaching her to trust him. They just needed some time.

Maybe it would help if he opened up a little first.

'I used to be married,' he said.

Bailey still looked wary, but at least she hadn't pulled away.

'I loved her. A lot. Sasha.' Funny, saying her name didn't make him feel as if he'd been put through the shredder any more. 'We were married for three years. I thought we were happy, but I guess she wanted more of a WAG lifestyle than I could give her—so that meant seeing a footballer rather than the team doctor.'

Bailey looked surprised. 'She left you for a footballer?'

Sasha had done a lot more than that, but Jared wasn't quite ready to talk about that bit. About how she'd totally shattered his world. How she'd had an affair, got pregnant, decided she didn't actually know who the father of her baby was as she'd been sleeping with them both, and had a termination without even telling him. 'Yes,' he said. 'She'd been seeing him for a while.'

'That's hard,' Bailey said.

He shrugged. 'It was at the time. But it was a couple of years ago now and I'm over it. We could probably just about be civil to each other if we were in the same room.'

'It's easier when you can be civil to each other,' she said.

'You're on civil terms with your ex now?'

* * *

It was her own fault, Bailey thought. She'd practically invited the question.

And she had to be honest with Jared. 'It wasn't Ed's fault that we broke up.' She'd shut her husband out and pushed him away. Sex had been out of the question because the fear of getting pregnant and having another ectopic pregnancy had frozen her. Ed had tried to get through to her, but her barriers had been too strong. And so he'd given up and turned elsewhere for comfort. She couldn't blame him for that. She hadn't been in love with him any more, but the way her marriage had ended still made her sad. 'Jared, I don't want to talk about it. Not right now.' She wriggled off his lap. 'And I think I ought to go home.'

'I'll drive you. I only had one glass of wine so I'm under the limit.'

'I'll be fine on the Tube,' she said. 'To be honest, I could do with a bit of a walk to clear my head.'

'Would you at least let me walk you to the Tube station?'

She shook her head. 'I'll be fine. But thank you—that was a really nice meal, and I appreciate it.'

And she needed to get out of here now, before she did something really stupid—like resting her head on his shoulder and crying all over him. It wouldn't be fair to dump her baggage on him, and it really wasn't fair to lead him on and let him think that this thing between them was going anywhere, because it couldn't happen. She wasn't sure she was ready to get that involved with someone again—especially someone who'd been hurt in the past and had his own baggage to deal with. She was attracted to Jared, seriously attracted, but that just wasn't enough to let her take that risk. She didn't want it all to go wrong and for him to get hurt because of her.

When Bailey still hadn't texted him by lunchtime the next day, Jared knew that he'd have to make the first move.

But what had spooked her?

She'd flatly refused to talk about it, so it had to be something huge. He wasn't sure how to get her to talk to him without making her put even more barriers up.

In the end, he called her. He half expected her to let the call go through to voicemail, but she answered. 'Hi, Jared.'

'How are you doing?' he asked softly.

'OK. Thanks for asking.'

'Want to go and get an ice cream or something?'

'Thanks, but I have a pile of work to do.'

It was an excuse, and he knew it. He could hear the panic in her voice, so he kept his tone calm and sensible. 'So if you have a lot of work to do, a short break will help refresh you.'

She sighed. 'You're not going to let this go, are you?'

'Nope,' he agreed.

'OK. What time?'

'Now?' he suggested. 'It's a nice afternoon.'

'Are you standing outside my flat or something?' she asked.

He laughed. 'No. I'm sitting in my kitchen, drinking coffee. Which is the alternative offer if you don't want ice cream.'

'You're pushy.'

'No. I'm not letting you push me away, and it's a subtle but important difference. I like you, Bailey,' he said. 'I think you and I could make a good team.'

There was a pause, and for a moment he thought he'd gone too far. But then she said, 'I like you, too.'

It was progress. Of sorts.

'I'll see you here in, what, an hour?' she asked.

'An hour's fine,' he said.

Jared turned up with flowers. Nothing hugely showy, nothing that made a statement or made Bailey feel under pressure; just a simple bunch of pretty yellow gerbera. 'They made me think of you,' he said.

Funny how that made her feel warm all over.

'Thank you. They're lovely.' She kissed his cheek, very quickly, and her mouth tingled at the touch of his skin. 'I'll put these in water.' Which was the perfect excuse for her to back away, and she was pretty sure he knew it, too.

They ended up going for a walk in the nearby park. And when Jared's fingers brushed against hers for the third time Bailey gave in and let him hold her hand. He didn't say a word about it, just chatted easily to her, and Bailey knew they'd turned another corner. That she was letting him closer, bit by bit.

Everything was fine until they walked past the children's play area.

'I used to take my niece to the park when she was small. Before she grew into a teen who's surgically attached to her mobile phone,' Jared said. 'The swings were her favourite. That and feeding the ducks.'

So that picture back at his place was of his niece. Even though Bailey's mouth felt as if it was full of sawdust, she had to ask the question. She needed to know the answer. Clearly he loved being an uncle—but would that be enough for him? 'Do you want children of your own?'

'Yes,' he said. 'I'd love to have kids—someone to kick a ball round with and read bedtime stories to. One day.'

Was it her imagination, or did he sound wistful? She didn't quite dare look at him. Besides, panic was flooding through her again.

He wanted children.

OK. So this thing between them was new. Fragile. There were no guarantees that things would work out. But it wouldn't be fair of her to let things go forward without at least telling him about her ectopic pregnancy. If he wanted kids, he needed to know that might not be an option for her. Yet, at the same time it felt too soon to raise the subject. As if she were presuming things.

She'd have to work out how to tell him. And when.

'What about you?' he asked.

How did she even begin answering that?

It was true. She did want children. But that would mean getting pregnant, and the whole idea of that terrified her. It was a vicious circle, and she didn't know how to break it. 'One day,' she said. Wanting to head him off the subject, she added, 'The café's just over there. The ice cream's on me.'

To her relief, he didn't argue or push the subject further. But he didn't let her hand go, either. He was just *there*. Warm and solid and dependable, not putting any pressure on her.

So maybe, she thought, they might have a chance.

She just had to learn to stop being scared.

CHAPTER NINE

EVERYTHING WAS FINE until the following Monday, when Bailey was having her usual chicken salad with Joni after the yoga class.

Joni had been a bit quiet all evening, looking worried.

'Is everything OK?' Bailey asked.

'Ye-es.'

But she didn't sound too sure. Bailey reached across the table and squeezed her hand. 'What? You've had a fight with Aaron? It happens. One or both of you is being an idiot, one or both of you will apologise and it'll be fine.'

'It's not that.' Joni bit her lip and there were tears in her eyes. 'Bailey, I don't know how to say this—I mean, it's good news, but I also know that...'

At that moment Bailey knew exactly what her best friend was going to tell her. And, even though it was ripping the top off her scars, no way in this world was she ever going to do anything other than smile—and she was going to try and make this easy for Joni, because she knew exactly why her best friend was worried about telling her. 'Joni, are you about to tell me something really, really fantastic—that you and Aaron are going to be…?'

The sheer relief in Joni's eyes nearly broke her.

'I've been dying to tell you since before the wedding, but…'

Yeah. Bailey could remember how it felt. The moment she'd suspected she was pregnant, the moment she'd done the test and seen the positive result, the way Ed had scooped her up and swung her round when she'd shown him the test stick. The sheer joy and happiness of knowing that they were going to have a baby, start their own family… She'd managed to keep the news to herself for four whole days before it had been too much to keep it in any more; she'd sworn both her mum and her best friend to total secrecy and had burst into happy tears when she'd told them. And whilst Ed had been worried about her jinxing it by telling everyone too early and not waiting until the twelve-week point was up, she'd been so happy that she just couldn't contain her news any longer.

Maybe Ed was right—maybe she *had* jinxed it by telling everyone too soon.

She pushed the thought away. Not now. This was about her best friend's future, not the wreck of her own past.

'Oh, Joni, I'm so pleased for you.' And she was, she really was. Just because it had gone bad for her, it didn't mean that she couldn't appreciate anyone else's joy. 'That's fantastic news. How far are you?'

'Ten weeks. I went for the dating scan today,' Joni said almost shyly.

'Good.' So Joni definitely wasn't going to go through the pain and fear of an ectopic pregnancy. Bailey almost sagged back in her chair in relief. 'So do I get to see a photograph, then?'

'Are you sure you want to see it?'

At that, Bailey got up, walked round to the other side of the table and hugged her friend. 'Don't be so daft! Of course I want to see the scan picture—I'd be really upset if you didn't show me.'

Joni blinked away tears. 'Sorry. I just didn't want to bring back…you know. And I'm being so wet.'

'Hormones,' Bailey said with a grin. 'You'll be crying at ads with puppies and kittens in them next.'

She sat down again as Joni reached into her bag for a little white folder and handed it to her. She studied the ultrasound photograph. 'You can see the baby's head, the feet, the spine— this is incredible, Joni.'

'And the heart—it was amazing to see the baby's heart beating.'

Bailey hadn't even got to do that bit, so it wasn't as if this was bringing back memories; it was more the shadow of what might have been. And she wasn't going to let any shadows get in the way of her best friend's joy. She was fiercely determined to share that joy with her.

'Bailey, there's something else I wanted to ask you,' Joni said. 'Will you be godmother?'

'Of course I will! I'd be utterly thrilled.' Bailey blanked out the fact that she'd wanted Joni to be godmother to her baby, too. 'So that means I get to do all the fun things, all the cuddles and the smiles and the messy toys, and then I hand the baby back to you for nappy changes and the night feeds. Excellent.'

She could see in Joni's eyes that her best friend knew exactly how much effort this was costing her and how much she was holding back, but to her relief Joni didn't say it. She simply smiled and said, 'Bailey Randall, you're going to be the best godmother in the history of the universe.'

'You can count on that,' Bailey said. 'And you can still do yoga during pregnancy, though maybe...' She took a deep breath. 'Maybe you need to switch to a water-aerobics class, one of the special antenatal ones. And I'll do it with you for moral support.'

She meant it, she really did—even though it would be hard seeing all those women with their bellies getting bigger each week and trying not to think about how that hadn't happened for her.

Joni reached across the table and squeezed her hand. 'I know you would. This is yet another reason why I love you. But I'm not going to make you do that. I'll stick to yoga—I'll talk to Jenna before the next class and ask her where I need to take it down a notch.'

Bailey kept it together at the restaurant, but all the way home she could feel the pressure behind her eyes, the sobs starting down low in her gut and forcing themselves upwards. Once her front door was closed behind her, she leaned against the wall and slowly slid down until she was sitting with her knees up to her chin and her arms wrapped round her legs. Then and only then did she let the tears flow—racking sobs of loss and loneliness, regrets for what might have been.

She didn't hear the doorbell at first. She was dimly aware of a noise then recognised the sound. Who was it? She wasn't expecting anyone. She scrubbed at her face with her sleeve and took a deep breath. Right at that moment she wished she hadn't cut her hair short, because then at least she could've hidden her face a bit. As it was, she'd have to brazen it out. She opened the door just a crack. 'Yes?'

'Bailey, are you all right?'

'Jared?' She frowned. 'What are you doing here?'

'We have a meeting to discuss Darren, remember?'

She remembered now. Joni's news had knocked the meeting completely out of her head.

She couldn't let Jared see her in this state. 'Can we do it tomorrow?'

'Are you all right?' he asked again, and this time he pushed the door open. He took one look at her and said, 'No, you're not all right.' Very gently, he manoeuvred her backwards, closed the door behind them and cupped her face between his hands. 'You've been crying.'

'Give the monkey a peanut,' she muttered,

knowing that she was being rude and unfair to him but hating the fact that he'd caught her at a weak, vulnerable moment.

But he didn't pay any attention to her words. 'Come on. I'll get you a drink of water.' He put one arm round her. 'Your kitchen's at the end of the corridor, yes?'

'Yes.'

She let him lead her into the kitchen and sit her down at the bistro table. He opened several cupboard doors before he found where she kept her glasses, then poured her a glass of water; she accepted it gratefully.

Jared waited until Bailey had composed herself for a bit before he made her talk. He knew she'd been to yoga with Joni and then out for dinner; it was their regular Monday night catchup. But he'd wanted to have a quick chat with Bailey about Darren, their problem player, so she'd agreed to be home for nine o'clock and meet him at her place. Jared had been caught up in a delay on the Tube after a signal had broken down, so he'd been all ready to apologise for being twenty minutes late for their meeting, but that didn't matter any more. Clearly something bad had just happened.

'What's happened? Is Joni all right?'

'She's fine.' Bailey dragged in a breath. 'It was good news.'

'Good news doesn't normally make you cry or look as if you've been put through the wringer,' he pointed out.

'I'm fine.'

They both knew she was lying.

'It's better out than in,' he said softly. And he should know. He'd bottled it up for a while after Sasha, until his oldest brother had read him the Riot Act and made him go to counselling. And that had made all the difference.

'I can't break a confidence.'

'Under the circumstances, I think,' he said softly, 'that Joni would forgive you. Or maybe I can guess. Good news, from someone who's just got married—it doesn't take a huge leap of the imagination to know what that's likely to be.'

And it didn't take a huge leap of the imagination to put the rest of it together, either. What would make someone bawl their eyes out when they learned that their best friend was going to have a baby? Either Bailey couldn't have children or she'd had a baby and lost it. Miscarriage, stillbirth, cot death…a loss so heartbreaking that she'd never really recovered from it. And neither had her marriage.

Was that why she'd been so adamant that the break-up hadn't been her ex's fault? And was that why she'd suddenly been so antsy at the park, when she'd asked him if he wanted children?

The way she looked at him, those beautiful dark eyes so tortured, was too much for him. He came round to her side of the table, scooped her out of her chair, sat in her place and settled her on his lap, his arms tightly wrapped round her. 'I'm not going anywhere until you talk to me. And whatever you say isn't going any further than me, I promise you.'

She didn't really know him well enough to

be completely sure that he wouldn't break his promise, but he hoped that she'd got to know him enough over the time they'd worked together to work out that he had integrity.

'What happened, Bailey?' What had broken her heart?

'I was pregnant once,' she whispered.

He stroked her face. 'When?'

'Two and a half years ago. I was so thrilled. We both were. We wanted that baby so much.'

He said nothing, just holding her close and waiting for her to tell him the rest.

'And then I started getting pains. In my lower abdomen. It hurt so much, Jared. I was worried that I might be having a miscarriage. And my shoulder hurt—but I assumed that was because I was worried.'

Jared knew that when you were stressed and tense you tended to hold yourself more rigidly and the muscles of your shoulder and neck would go into spasm, causing shoulder pain. Clearly that hadn't been the reason for the pain in this case.

'I went to the toilet,' she said, 'and there was spotting.' She closed her eyes. 'I felt sick. Light-headed.' She dragged in a breath. 'Then I collapsed. Luckily one of my colleagues found me and they got me in to the department. I told them I was pregnant, but I knew what was happening. I *knew*.'

A miscarriage? Heartbreaking for her.

'They gave me a scan. I was six weeks and three days. The pregnancy was ectopic.'

Even harder than he'd guessed. The fertilised egg hadn't implanted into the uterus, the way it should've done. Instead, it had embedded in the Fallopian tube and stretched the tube as it had grown, causing Bailey's lower abdominal pain.

'My Fallopian tube had ruptured. They took me straight into Theatre,' she said, 'but they couldn't save the tube.' Her voice wobbled, and then a shudder ran through her. 'I wanted that baby so much. And I—I...'

'Shh, I know.' He stroked her hair. 'And it wasn't your fault.' It happened in something like one out of eighty pregnancies. Often it sorted itself out and the woman hadn't even known she was pregnant in the first place. But Bailey had been unlucky, caught up in one of the worst-case scenarios.

And clearly the fact her best friend had just shared the news of her pregnancy had brought it all back. Joni had doubtless been one of the first people that Bailey had told about her own pregnancy, and Jared would just bet that Joni had agonised over telling her best friend the news, knowing that it would bring all these excruciating memories back. And he was equally sure that Bailey had gone into super-sparkly mode to reassure her that it was fine, all the while her heart breaking into tiny pieces again.

'The ectopic pregnancy wasn't my fault,' Bailey said, 'but the rest of it was.'

The rest of it? He'd obviously spoken aloud without meaning to, or maybe the question was just obvious, because she started talking again.

'I pushed Ed away afterwards. I—I just couldn't cope with the idea of it happening all over again.'

Jared knew that a second ectopic pregnancy was more likely if you'd had a first. He'd never worked in obstetrics, but he was pretty sure that the statistics weren't shockingly high. Bailey's fears had obviously got the better of her.

'I was so scared of getting pregnant again. So scared of losing another baby. So scared of losing my other Fallopian tube, so I'd never be able to have a baby without medical intervention. I wouldn't let Ed touch me. I knew he was hurting and he needed me, but I just *couldn't* let him touch me. I couldn't give him the physical comfort he wanted.' She leaned her head against his shoulder. 'I was such a selfish bitch.'

'You were hurting, too, Bailey,' he reminded her softly. 'You weren't being selfish. You were hurting and you didn't know how to fix it—for yourself or for your husband.'

'In the end, Ed found comfort elsewhere. But he—he wasn't like your ex,' she whispered. 'He wasn't out there looking for someone else. He would never have done it if I hadn't pushed him away and made him feel as if I didn't care. It was all my fault.'

And now he understood why her family worried about her so much and were so keen for her to meet someone. Not because she was 'on the shelf', but because they knew how much she'd been through and they wanted her to find someone to share her life with and to cherish her, someone who'd stop her being lonely and sad.

If she'd let him, maybe he could do that. Maybe they could both help each other heal.

But Bailey had pushed her husband away, terrified of getting pregnant again. She'd ended her marriage rather than risk another pregnancy going wrong.

And that explained why she'd responded to him and then backed off again so swiftly. She'd felt the pull of attraction between them just as much as he had, but she was too scared to act on it. Too scared to date, to grow intimate with him, to make love with him—in case she became pregnant and she ended up having another ectopic pregnancy.

'It takes two to break a marriage,' he said. 'Your ex gave up on you.'

'You gave up on your marriage,' she pointed out.

He knew she'd only said it because she was hurting. Clearly she thought that sniping at him would make him walk away and leave her to it. Maybe that was one of the tactics she'd used to push her husband away, but it wasn't going to work on him. 'Yes, I did,' he said. 'I'll take my share of the blame. Just as long as you accept that not all the blame of your break-up is yours.'

'It feels like it is,' she said, sounding totally broken.

If only he had a magic wand. But this wasn't something he could fix. The only one who could let her trust again, let her take the risk of sharing her life with someone, was Bailey herself. Until she was ready to try, it just wouldn't work.

So he said nothing, just held her. If necessary, he'd stay here all night, just cradling her on his lap and hoping she'd be able to draw some strength from the feel of her arms around him.

Eventually, she stroked his face. 'Thank you, Jared. For listening. And for not judging.'

Unable to help himself, he twisted his face round so he could drop a kiss into her palm. 'No worries.'

'I'm sorry I cried all over you.'

'It probably did you good,' he said.

'And we were supposed to be talking about Darren,' she said.

He smiled. 'Don't worry about it. Darren can wait. We'll talk about him tomorrow, maybe. Right now, this is a bit more important.'

'I don't normally cry over people.'

No. He'd guess that normally she sparkled that little bit more brightly, pretending everything was fine and waiting until she was on her own before letting her true feelings show. 'It's fine. Really.'

'I, um, ought to let you go. It's getting late.'

'I'm not going anywhere,' he said softly.

'But...'

'Bailey, do you really think I can walk away

and just leave you here alone, upset and hurting?' he asked.

She just looked at him, those huge, huge eyes full of pain.

'It's your choice,' he said. 'I can sleep on your sofa tonight—just so I know you're not alone, and I'm here if you need anything. Or...' He paused.

'Or?' she whispered.

'Or I can hold you until you fall asleep. Sleep with you.'

Even though she tried to hide it, he could see the panic flood into her face. 'I said *sleep*, Bailey,' he reminded her quietly. 'Which isn't the same as having sex.'

'I—I'm sorry.'

He kissed the corner of her mouth. 'You're upset, you're trying to be brave and all your nightmares have come back to haunt you. Some people might use sex as a way of escaping it all, but you're not one of them. And I would never push you into anything you're not happy with.'

'I know.' She swallowed hard. 'I'm a mess,

Jared. And you've been hurt in the past, too. I'm the last person you need to get involved with.'

'Let me be the judge of that,' he said gently. 'And let me be here for you tonight.'

Bailey knew it was a genuine offer. It would be, oh, so easy to take him up on it. To lean on him. To take comfort from the warmth of his body curled round hers.

But it would also make things really complicated.

'You're going to be stubborn about this, aren't you?' he asked wryly.

She nodded. 'And you said I had a choice.'

'Sofa?' he asked.

'Go home,' she said. 'Really. I'll be fine.'

'How about we compromise?' Jared suggested. 'You let me hold you—on the sofa—until you're asleep. Then I'll tuck you in and I'll leave—though if you wake at stupid o'clock and you need to talk, then you call me.'

So, so generous. She stroked his face. 'I'm sorry I called you Herod.'

He smiled. 'That was the autocorrect on your phone.'

'But I never took it back. And you're not a tyrant at all. You're more like Sir Galahad. A knight on a white charger coming to the rescue.'

He laughed. 'Hardly. I'm just a man, Bailey.'

'There's no "just". You're a good man, Jared Fraser. Kind. You do all that gruff, dour Scotsman stuff—but that's the opposite of who you really are.'

'Thank you,' he said. 'Now lead me to your sofa.'

'Don't you want a drink or anything? I've been horribly rude and haven't even offered you a coffee.'

He kissed the tip of her nose. 'In the circumstances, that's not so surprising. And I don't want a coffee. I just want to hold you until you fall asleep.'

'Yes,' she said softly, and led him through to the sofa in her living room.

CHAPTER TEN

THE NEXT MORNING, Bailey woke to find herself still fully clothed on the sofa, with her duvet tucked round her.

Falling asleep in Jared's arms last night had felt risky—but it had also felt so, so good.

She grabbed her phone, but a wave of unexpected shyness stopped her calling him. What would she even say?

Instead, she sent him a text: Thank you for last night.

Her phone pinged almost immediately with his reply: No worries. Sleep well?

Yes. Thank you.

Good. See you at work. And this time he'd signed his text with a kiss.

Maybe this was going to work out after all. Jared made her feel brave. And his ex, Bailey thought, really needed her head examined. Why would you throw away the love of a kind, decent, thoughtful man for a shallow, publicity-obsessed lifestyle?

Then again, unhappiness made you do stupid things. Cruel things. Bailey knew she was just as guilty when it came to the way she'd pushed Ed away. And didn't they say you shouldn't judge someone until you'd walked a mile in their shoes?

She showered, changed and headed for the football pitch. But when she got there she was surprised to find that the players weren't warming up as usual on the field. Instead, they were sitting in the dressing room, and the mood was extremely subdued.

'What's the matter, lads?' she asked.

'You need to go in and see Mr Fincham in his office,' Billy said. 'Archie and Jared are already there.'

Mr Fincham? Why would the football club's chairman of directors want to see her? 'Why?' she asked.

'I can't say.' He bit his lip. 'But there's trouble, Bailey.'

Worried, Bailey hurried along to the office. Mandy, Lyle Fincham's PA, was typing furiously on her keyboard. 'Mandy, what's going on?' Bailey asked.

Mandy shook her head. 'That's for Mr Fincham to say, not me.' She inclined her head towards the door. 'They're in there, waiting. You'd better go in.'

Bailey knocked on the door out of courtesy and walked in. 'Sorry I'm a bit late. There was a delay on the Tube.'

Then she saw Darren sitting between Archie and Jared. And Jared was looking every inch the dour, unsmiling Scotsman.

'It's in all the papers this morning,' Lyle said, indicating the stack of newspapers on his desk. 'And all over the Internet.'

'What is?' she asked.

'The video of laddo here.' Lyle jerked his head towards Darren. 'In a club, getting drunk. Underage.'

She looked at Darren, who was white-faced and looked utterly guilty. So much for making the most of his second chance. Or maybe they just hadn't given him enough support. After all, Jared had originally wanted to talk to her last night about the boy; they hadn't got round to discussing the situation, because she'd been in meltdown.

And yet…something didn't quite stack up. The last couple of weeks, since she'd picked up Darren's underperformance and she and Jared had persuaded Archie to give the boy another chance, his stats had all been back to normal. 'When did all this happen?' she asked.

'Last night,' Archie said grimly.

Darren shook his head. 'I wasn't out last night. You can ask my mum. She'll tell you.'

'Actually, my stats show that Darren's performance has been normal ever since we talked to you, Archie,' Bailey said. 'If he'd still been drinking, it would've shown up on my graphs.'

'Graphs, schmaphs,' Lyle Fincham said, flapping a dismissive hand. 'Archie should never have let that box of tricks of yours cloud his judgement. This is a total mess, and I can't afford to let this affect the club. As from today, you're out, Dr Randall. I don't care how much of your research project's wasted. It's over.'

'Actually, I agree with Bailey,' Jared cut in. 'It would show on the graphs. And if she goes, I go.'

No. No way was she letting Jared risk his career. For her, this was a research project. Yes, there would be repercussions about the way it had ended, but it would eventually blow over. For Jared, it would be his whole career on the line. This wasn't fair.

'I was the one who talked Archie into giving Darren another chance, so don't take this out on Jared,' she said swiftly. 'Don't make him leave because of me.'

'And that video's from weeks back, I swear. I haven't touched a drop since you said I could stay, Mr McLennan,' Darren added desperately, giving Archie a beseeching look. 'I know I was stupid to do it before.'

'But you've still dragged the club's name into disrepute.' Lyle shook his head. 'No. You're out, boy, so go and pack your things.'

'That's not fair—he's owned up to his mistakes, and this is just bad timing,' Bailey said. 'Nobody's perfect. Can you honestly put your hand on your heart and say that you've never, ever made a decision you haven't later regretted?'

Lyle gave her a speaking look.

'We all have the potential to make the wrong choice somewhere along the way. It's hard to own up to it. But Darren admitted his mistake and he's doing something about it.' Bailey grimaced. 'Look, can Darren just go and wait in another room while we talk about this like the professionals we are? It's horrible, all of us standing round like vultures pecking at the poor lad.'

'I agree,' Jared chipped in. 'And I also think we can turn this around so the club can make this a positive. We'll need your PR manager to help us, but we can do it.'

For a moment, she thought Lyle Fincham was going to refuse, but then he tightened his mouth and nodded. 'Darren, go and wait next door with Mandy. You don't move a muscle, you don't phone anyone or talk to anyone and you don't go anywhere near the Internet, do you hear? Leave your phone with us.'

Looking hunted, the boy handed over his phone and went to wait with Lyle's PA next door.

Lyle picked up his phone. 'Max? My office. Now. There's a situation that needs handling.' He put the phone down again. 'Right. So we'll sort this out between us.'

'Darren's only seventeen. He's still just a kid, really. He's not going to think things through properly, the way someone more mature would do. Instead of coming to you to ask about extra training, Archie, he got drunk to blot out how he felt. You agreed to give him a second chance. He's stayed clean since then—and I bet if you ask any of the other lads they'll be able to tell you that, too,' Bailey said.

'I let you persuade me into giving him another chance, yes,' Archie said. 'But if one player goes wrong, then all the players get tarred with the same brush. You know what the press is like about how much money is in football. They'll have a field day with the kid—and with the club. This isn't fair to the rest of the players, or to the fans.'

'Or the shareholders,' Lyle added. 'His behaviour's put everything at risk.'

'But we can turn this round,' Jared said. 'Really.'

There was a rap on the door and Max Porter, the PR manager, came in. 'So what's this situation?'

'Darren. There's a video of him drunk and underage.' Lyle's colour was dangerously high again, and Bailey was really beginning to worry that the chairman of directors was about to have a heart attack or a stroke.

'Right,' Max said calmly. 'Talk me through it.'

'We picked it up on Bailey's system,' Jared

said. 'He admitted he'd been drinking. Archie agreed to give him another chance.'

'And he hasn't touched anything since,' Bailey said. 'All his stats since we talked to him about it match his average. And it would show up if he was still drinking.'

'I've analysed the way he plays and designed a training programme to help him improve his weak spots,' Jared added.

'So you both obviously think he should stay,' Max said. Then he looked at Archie and Lyle. 'And I take it you both think he should go?'

'And not just him,' Lyle said with a pointed look at Jared and Bailey.

'We can turn this around,' Jared said again. 'This is a classic example of what the pressures of professional football can do to young players. We brought Darren into the club. We set the bar high. And what do we do with the players who can't handle the pressure? Do we just abandon them, in a cold-hearted business decision? Or do we treat them like a family member—knowing he has flaws, knowing he's human and helping him to get over the problem?'

'That's a good spin,' Max said. 'I do hope you're not planning to change career and go after my job, Jared.'

The joke was just enough to dissipate some of the tension in the room. *Just.*

'We don't just need to teach our young players ball skills,' Jared said. 'We need to teach them life skills, because this is a kind of apprenticeship and we're responsible for the way our players develop as people, not just as players. We need to show them how to own up to their mistakes and how to start to make things right.' He paused. 'When my knee was wrecked by that tackle, I was the same age as Darren and it felt like the end of the world, knowing I was never going to be able to play professional football again.'

Knowing how rarely he spoke about this, Bailey held her breath for a moment.

'I could so easily have gone off the rails,' Jared continued. 'But my family and my coach were brilliantly supportive. They stopped me doing anything stupid. And we need to do that for Darren.'

'Actually, Darren could be a good ambassador for the club,' Max said thoughtfully. 'We could get him to talk about his mistakes to kids at school, how he's overcome them and how he managed to get back on the right path with our help. They can learn from his mistakes rather than making those mistakes themselves.'

'So he gets away with it?' Lyle asked, his nostrils flaring in disgust.

'No. Because you could always fine him,' Bailey suggested. 'Donate the fine to a charity specialising in alcohol abuse among kids. Then his mistake will help people who also made mistakes.'

'Making the punishment fit the crime,' Archie said. 'I like that. And he's not a bad lad, Lyle. He's not wild. We need to give him a bit more pride in himself.'

'And what's the press going to think? That I

condone all sorts of nonsense at the club?' Lyle demanded.

'No. They'll think that you expect the best from people, but you don't just throw them to the wolves if they get it wrong. You help them be the best they can be,' Max said. 'You're going to get all the mums on your side.'

'Mums don't buy season tickets,' Lyle grumbled.

'Maybe, but they can talk their partners into buying a season ticket for a club that gives a damn about the kids and doesn't just see them as future cash cows,' Jared said.

Lyle threw his hands up. 'I give up. All right. The boy gets a second chance. But you make sure everyone knows we fined him for doing wrong, and that we donated that money to help kids who made the same mistake.'

'Thank you,' Bailey said. 'And I'm sorry I didn't talk it over with you and Archie. I understand why you don't want me here again after today.'

'You know, it would be a shame to lose all that

PR—it shows that we care so much about our players' well-being, we've worked with them using the latest technology to help reduce soft-tissue injuries,' Jared said, looking at Max and then Lyle.

'He's right,' Max said. 'It's a brilliant story and it would be a real pity to lose it.'

This time, Jared looked straight at Bailey. 'Everyone deserves a second chance,' he said softly.

She knew he didn't just mean Darren, or their work on the team. He meant them. A second chance to get it right. And it made her go hot all over.

'All right, all right,' Lyle grumbled. 'You can finish your research, Dr Randall. But one foot out of line from you in future…or you,' he warned, gesturing to Jared, 'and that's it.'

'I promise,' Bailey said.

'Me, too,' Jared said. 'Should we send Darren back in to learn his fate?'

'Do that,' Archie said, clapping them both on the back. 'And we'll postpone training until this afternoon. Two-thirty, sharp. Tell them for me, will you?'

* * *

Bailey and Jared went next door into Mandy's office. 'Darren, you can go back in now,' Jared said.

'What did Mr Fincham say?' Darren asked, looking anxious.

'He'll listen to you and be fair about it. Just go in, tell the truth and you'll be fine,' Bailey advised him.

Then they went into the dressing room to see the rest of the players. They were full of questions, all talking together and not giving anyone a chance to answer them.

'Has Darren been sacked?'

'Is the boss mad because of all the stuff that happened in that nightclub?'

'Are the rest of us going to be sacked?'

'Shh—calm down,' Bailey said. 'Archie will be in to see you later and he'll explain everything. In the meantime, training today has been postponed until two-thirty. I'm sure you lot have stuff you can get on with in the meantime—and stay out of trouble, OK?'

'Nicely done,' Jared said when they left the dressing room.

'I've got everyone into quite enough trouble as it is,' she said ruefully. 'And I'm sorry, Jared. I really thought you were going to lose your job because of me back there.'

'Lyle always blows up. He'll calm down again.' Jared gave her a wry smile. 'Though I was worrying about him back there. I didn't like his colour.'

'Me, neither,' she agreed.

'Maybe you could teach him some of your yoga stuff to help him relax and reduce his blood pressure.'

'Suggesting that,' she said, 'is probably more than my life's worth right now—and yours.'

'Well, it looks as if we have some unexpected free time.' He paused. 'Want some cake?'

'I think that's a really good idea,' she said.

'My place isn't far. And there's a good patisserie on the corner.'

'That sounds good to me,' she said. 'Though

I insist on buying, considering I nearly got you the sack.'

'No, you didn't—but I'm not going to turn down the offer of cake,' he said with a smile. 'Let's go.'

CHAPTER ELEVEN

THEY BOUGHT CAKE at the café and walked back to Jared's place in comfortable silence. Jared made them both a mug of coffee; Bailey was relieved that they sat in his kitchen, given how they'd ended up kissing on his sofa. She didn't quite trust herself not to repeat that, especially as the more time she spent with Jared, the more attractive she found him.

He'd hinted at a second chance. Did she dare take it?

'I was wondering,' he said, 'if you were doing anything at the weekend.'

'Nothing out of the ordinary,' she said. What did he have in mind? Adrenalin fizzed through her at the possibilities.

'I know it's ridiculously short notice, but there's this football function on Saturday night—a charity ball thing. I, um, have two tickets.'

'And you've been let down at the last minute?'

He frowned. 'Bailey, I'm not the kind of man who asks someone to go to a dinner with me and then kisses someone else stupid.'

'No, of course not.' But he was obviously remembering those kisses, too. Had he been planning to ask her to the ball all along? Or had he just bought the tickets to do his bit to support the charity, not actually intending to be there on the night?

She blew out a breath. 'Sorry. I didn't mean to insult you. Honestly. First I nearly lose you your job, and then I practically accuse you of being a philanderer... I'm not doing very well today.'

'The job thing was just as much my fault,' he said. 'And I think you and I...' He blew out a breath. 'It's complicated.'

'Just a tad.' She paused. 'So is this an official date? In public?'

He held her gaze. 'It could be. Or it could be

the same deal as you had with me at Joni and Aaron's wedding.'

A fake date, to take the heat off him?

'Sasha's going to be there?' she guessed.

'Possibly.' He shrugged. 'I have no idea.'

There was something she needed to know. 'Are you still in love with her?'

'No. Actually, I don't care whether she's there or not. That isn't the reason I asked you. I only bought the tickets to support the charity,' he admitted. 'I wasn't actually going to go.'

Just as she'd half suspected.

'But I've been thinking about it. And I'd like to go.' He paused. 'With you.'

It was tempting. So very tempting. And maybe the sugar rush of the cake was to blame for her opening her mouth and saying, 'Yes.'

His smile made her feel warm all over.

'So where do I meet you, and what time?' she asked.

'I could pick you up from your place at seven?' he suggested.

'That works for me.'

And how crazy it was that this made her feel like a teenager all over again.

A second chance. If you counted the wedding, this would be their third attempt at a date. At the wedding, and when they'd had dinner together, she'd ended up panicking and backing away. Would this be third time lucky? Would she be able to get over the fear this time?

Jared was a good man. He'd stuck up for her. He'd been there for her when she'd needed a shoulder. He ticked all her boxes. All she had to do was get rid of the fears inside her head.

All.

The training session that afternoon was pretty much as usual. The lads were a little subdued but did their best, including Darren. She was busy at clinic the rest of the week.

And all too soon Saturday night arrived.

Rather than going all out for a ballgown, Bailey had chosen a black lacy dress and patent black leather high heels. Simple yet sophisticated enough for the function, she hoped. And as soon as she opened the door to Jared, she knew from the flare of heat in his gaze that she'd made the right decision. He definitely liked what she was wearing.

'Hello,' she said, feeling ridiculously shy.

'You look fabulous,' he said softly.

'So do you.' She'd seen him in a suit before, but not a dinner jacket. How crazy that something as simple as a dark red bow tie should look so incredibly sexy on him. Just to stop herself doing something stupid—like grabbing him and kissing him and dragging him off to her bed instead of going to the ball—she said, 'Though I was half expecting you to wear a kilt.'

He laughed. 'That would be a wee bit clichéd.'

But, to her relief, laughter broke the tension just enough to get her common sense back.

Jared had seen Bailey dressed up before, but it did nothing to stop the shock of how attractive he found her. Right at that moment he didn't want to go to the charity ball and share her; he wanted her all to himself. He wanted to kiss her until they were both dizzy, and then take her to bed and spend the whole night finding out what gave her the most pleasure. But he held himself in check. Just.

He ushered her to the taxi. When he reached for her hand on the way to the dinner-dance, she curled her fingers round his.

Maybe, just maybe, this thing between them was going to go right.

At the dinner, Bailey went into sparkle mode. She chatted to absolutely everyone, not in the slightest bit fazed by the incredibly glamorous WAGs there or how famous some of the players were. But Jared noticed that she didn't only talk to the famous ones; she talked to everyone and drew them out.

Bailey Randall had a gift for making people feel special.

He watched her sparkle and thought, *I could really lose my heart to this woman.* He knew she was as special as she made people feel, but he also knew that she had a protective shell

round her. He wasn't sure if he'd be able to persuade her to let him past it.

He turned round to see Sasha there with her
third husband in tow. Jared had expected to feel
some kind of reaction at seeing her again—but
he was surprised and relieved to discover he
didn't. What had happened was in the past. It
couldn't be changed. And it didn't matter any
more—it didn't *hurt* any more.

And he knew why: because Bailey was in his
life. Being with Bailey made his world a much
brighter place.

After he'd introduced Bailey to Sasha and her
husband, Jared made his excuses and drew Bailey towards the dance floor.

'Are you OK?' Bailey asked.

'Sure. Why wouldn't I be?'

She coughed. 'Sasha's not exactly a common
name. I take it she's *the* Sasha.'

'Yes. Actually, I thought I'd find it difficult
to see her,' he admitted, 'but there's just nothing there any more. It's fine,' he reassured her.

But he also noticed that Bailey didn't look fine. 'What's wrong?' he asked softly.

'Well—she's incredibly beautiful.'

'And?' He didn't get it.

She shook her head. 'Nothing.'

Then he got it. And it surprised him that Bailey was feeling vulnerable. The Bailey Randall he'd got to know was incredibly together and was comfortable in her own skin, and he really liked that. 'I know you're not fishing for compliments,' he said, 'but, just for the record, you can more than hold your own with her. You're just as beautiful, except yours is a natural beauty.' He paused. 'And I'm so glad you're nothing like her as a person.'

'Hmm,' she said.

'Just to make it clear,' he said softly, 'right now I'm dating a woman I really, really like. A woman I respect for who she is.' He held her gaze. 'And whom I happen to find very, very attractive.'

Had he gone too far?

Panicking that he might make her back off,

he added, 'Anyway, your hair's shorter than Sasha's.'

'I used to wear it long.'

He held her closer. He could guess when she'd cut it. After she'd lost the baby. 'No shadows tonight,' he said softly. 'This is just you and me.' He pulled back slightly so she could see his eyes and know that he was telling the truth. 'I've put the past to rest.'

'Good.'

For a moment he wondered if she was going to say that she'd put her past to rest, too.

But she didn't. And he knew he was going to have to take this at her pace.

When he'd been younger he wouldn't have had the patience to do that. But Bailey Randall was going to be more than worth his patience, he thought. So he wasn't going to push her until she was ready.

During the evening, Bailey danced with both Lyle Fincham and Archie.

Archie tipped his head towards Jared. 'Are you and Jared…you know?'

She smiled. 'I'm taking the Fifth Amendment on that one.'

He laughed. 'You can't. You're not American.'

'I'm still doing it. Anyway, under English law you have the right to remain silent, too,' she pointed out.

'I guess.' He smiled. 'He's a good man. I know you two didn't exactly hit it off at first.'

'Jared's not the grumpy Scotsman he likes everyone to think he is,' she said with a grin.

'Exactly. And I think you'll be good together.'

'It's early days, Archie,' she said softly. She wasn't quite ready to believe this was all going to work out. But she really was going to try and put the past behind her.

Eventually Jared claimed Bailey back. Perfect timing, too, because the music changed to soft and slow, which meant that she was right where he wanted her—up close and personal. And she was holding him just as tightly. He wasn't going to embarrass her by kissing her stupid in public, but maybe…

'Shall we get out of here?' he murmured into her ear. 'Go and have a glass of wine back at my place?'

He didn't realise he was holding his breath until she said yes.

He held her hand in the taxi all the way back to his place.

And once the front door was closed behind him, he was able to do what he'd wanted to do all evening and kiss her.

He could drown in her warmth and sweetness.

He broke this kiss before he did something stupid, like carrying her upstairs to his bed. Too fast, too soon. 'I promised you a glass of wine,' he said hoarsely.

'I don't really want a drink,' she said softly.

Then what did she want?

Anticipation thrummed through him. Did she want the same thing that he did? Did she want to lose herself in him, the way he wanted to lose himself in her?

'Last time I was here, you put pictures in my head,' she said. 'Do you happen to have any more of that fabulous chocolate pudding?'

'No, but I can improvise,' he said. Then he went very still as he took in what she'd just said. Not quite sure he'd got this right, he asked, 'Bailey, are you saying we can…?'

'Yes. Provided,' she said, 'we're really careful and you use protection. I'm not on the Pill. I never thought I'd…' She tailed off, wrinkling her nose and looking awkward.

He knew what she meant. When she'd told him about her ectopic pregnancy, she'd also told him how scared she was of getting pregnant again and how she'd pushed her husband away physically. And so what she was offering him now was *hugely* brave. So generous it made him catch his breath. She was going to trust him. To let him prove to her that having sex again wasn't going to make her life implode. 'I'll take care of you,' he said softly, 'and I want you so badly it hurts—but I know this is really scary for you. If you change your mind at any point tonight and say you want to stop, that's also fine. We can take this as slowly as you like.'

Tears glittered in her eyes. 'Thank you, Jared.'

He needed to ask. 'Do you want me to stop now?'

She took a deep breath. 'Yes. And no. Both at the same time. I'm scared, Jared,' she admitted.

'I know. And I understand.' He held her close for a moment. 'But maybe, just maybe, you can be brave with me. Maybe we can be brave with each other,' he said, and drew her hand to his mouth. He kissed each fingertip in turn, then her palm, folding her fingers over his kiss.

She stood on tiptoe and kissed the end of his nose. And then the corner of his mouth. And then she caught his lower lip between hers, in silent demand that they deepen the kiss.

He was more than happy to comply. And happier still when she kissed him back, matching him touch for touch and nibble for nibble.

'I want you,' he whispered. 'So very, very badly.'

'I want you, too,' she said, her voice low and husky and sensual.

He didn't need a second invitation. He scooped her up and carried her up the stairs to his bedroom. He'd already closed the curtains before he'd left that evening, so all he had to deal with was the light, once he'd set her back down on her feet.

In the soft light of the table lamp he could see the strain on her face. The fear.

'It's OK,' he said. 'We can stop.'

She shook her head. 'Not now.'

'Are you sure?'

She took a deep breath. 'I'm sure.'

He knew she wasn't yet she was clearly trying to push herself past the fear. So he'd do what he could to help. He kissed her lightly, then slid the zip at the back of her dress all the way down. He pushed the lacy material off her shoulders and the dress slid to the floor. She stepped out of it, and he hung it over the back of a chair, not wanting the dress to be spoiled. And then he held her at arm's length. 'You take my breath away, Bailey,' he said huskily.

'Right now,' she said, with the tiniest wobble in her voice that told him she was still panicking inside, 'I think I'd feel a bit better if you weren't wearing quite so much.'

He smiled. 'I'm all yours. Do what you will with me.'

She slid his jacket off and placed it over her dress on the chair. Then she checked his bow tie. He could see the moment that she realised it was a proper one. 'Very flash,' she said, rolling her eyes, and pulled both ends. The knot came apart in her hands, and she draped the tie over his jacket.

Next was his shirt, and he noticed that her hands were slightly unsteady as she undid the buttons. She pushed the material off his shoulders. 'Oh, your biceps,' she breathed, and stroked the muscles. 'I've wanted to do this since we trained together. They're so beautiful.'

And so was she. He needed to see her. Properly. All of her. 'Can I play caveman now?' he asked. Stupid, because he'd already done that by carrying her up the stairs.

'I was thinking superhero,' she said. 'One with really, really sexy biceps. Though I can live with the fact you're not wearing a cape.'

'That works for me.' At her nod, he unclipped her bra and turned her round. 'Oh, my God, Bailey. You're glorious.' He kissed his way down her spine. 'If I could paint, I'd want you to model for me.' He stroked her back. 'You're perfect.' He drew her back against him so she could feel his erection pressing against her and would know that he meant every word of what he said. He cupped her breasts and kissed the curve of her shoulder. 'Right now, I want you so badly. You make me ache, Bailey. In a good way.'

She turned round in his arms. 'Then take me to bed, Jared.'

He didn't need her to ask again. He picked her up and carried her to the bed, then laid her gently against the covers.

* * *

Time seemed to stop. Bailey wasn't sure which of them had removed the rest of his clothes and her underwear, but finally they were skin to skin.

Then she froze as she realised what was just about to happen. She wanted this—she really, really did—but supposing this all went wrong?

'Stop thinking, Bailey,' he whispered. 'Let yourself go. Let yourself *feel*.'

He kissed her again; she tipped her head back against the pillows, and he kissed the curve of her throat, lingering in the hollows of her collarbones.

She could feel her nipples tightening; he nuzzled his way down her sternum and then took one nipple into his mouth, sucking hard. Bailey pushed her hands through his hair, urging him on, and his mouth moved lower, lower.

She almost forgot how to breathe when she felt the long, slow stroke of his tongue along her sex. And it was like a starburst in her head when he teased her clitoris with the tip of his tongue. Her climax was shockingly fast. Oh, God. She'd forgotten what this was like. For-gotten how it felt. Forgotten how good it could be. And it had been so long…

He waited until the aftershocks had died away, then came up to lie beside her and drew her into his arms. 'OK?'

'I think so,' she said. 'Which planet am I on again?'

He chuckled softly. 'I wanted that first time to be all for you.'

He cared that much? She felt a single tear leak out of the corner of her eye.

He kissed it away. 'Bailey, I think we're going to be good together.'

The panic threatened to spill over again, but she pushed it away. She'd said that she'd be brave with him. She wasn't going to back out now.

'Show me,' she whispered.

He took a condom from his drawer and handed her the packet. 'You're in control.'

She knew exactly why he'd done that—so

she could be quite, quite sure that there was no chance of getting pregnant, because she'd know they'd used the condom properly—and had to blink back the tears, but she ripped open the packet and rolled the condom over his shaft. And then finally, finally, he was inside her. He held himself very still so her body could adjust to the feel of him, then began to move.

He was a concentrated lover, she discovered. One who didn't talk and who focused on his goals. And, oh, having that focus entirely on her… She was aware of every touch, every kiss, and she knew that he was exploring her and paying very, very close attention to what she liked, and what she liked even more.

It shouldn't be this good. Not their first time. It should be awkward and embarrassing and faintly ridiculous.

But then she stopped thinking as she felt a climax spiralling through her again. She clung onto him for dear life and knew the very second that he'd fallen over the edge, too.

When they'd both floated back to earth, he

moved. 'I'd better deal with the condom,' he said softly, and kissed her shoulder. 'Stay there. You look comfortable.' She *was* comfortable. And even though there was a slow burn of panic deep inside her, knowing that Jared was there— that he was solid and dependable and real— helped her to ignore that panic. It was time she stopped letting what had happened to her dictate her life. Time she stopped letting it scare her away from what she wanted. With Jared by her side, supportive and compassionate, she could have everything.

That night, she fell asleep in his arms, just as she had on her sofa. But this time when she woke she was still in his arms. In his bed. Skin to skin. Warm and comfortable. She kept her eyes closed for a little while longer, just luxuriating in the feeling of being held. Of being cherished. She'd forgotten how good this could be.

'Good morning,' he said softly when she opened her eyes at last.

'Yes. It is,' she said with a smile. 'Because you're here.'

'It's the same for me. I don't care if it's raining outside, because it feels like the brightest summer day.' He stroked her face. 'So will you stay for breakfast?'

She kissed him lightly. 'Thank you. I'd love to.'

He made her pancakes with maple syrup and some truly excellent coffee. They went back to her flat so she could change from her lacy cocktail dress into something casual, and spent the rest of the day wandering hand in hand along the South Bank, enjoying the market stalls and the art installations and the street performers.

'No regrets?' he said on her doorstep when he finally saw her home.

'None,' she said. 'Today's been fantastic. Actually, it's the first time in a long while that I've felt this happy.'

'Me, too,' he said.

'So I was wondering,' she said. 'I'm not promising pancakes, but I make a mean bacon sandwich.'

His eyes widened. 'Are you asking me to stay for breakfast, Bailey?'

She took a deep breath. 'Yes.'

'Sure?' he checked.

'It still scares me a bit, the idea of having another relationship,' she admitted. 'But yes. You make me feel brave. I can do this, with you.'

In answer, he kissed her. And she opened her front door and ushered him inside.

CHAPTER TWELVE

FOR THE NEXT three weeks Bailey was really happy. She and Jared were so in tune—and she really liked the funny, kind, gentle man beneath his dour exterior. She also enjoyed the occasional sarcastic text he sent her, signed 'Herod'. He was never going to let her forget that, was he?

This was all still so new that she wasn't quite ready to share it with her family or her best friend, but she found herself looking forward to every evening that she spent with Jared, every night that she slept in his arms and every morning that she woke and he was the first one she saw.

Work was fantastic. She'd always enjoyed her clinic work, and she'd been accepted as one of the team at the football club, so both strands of her job suited her perfectly.

Life didn't get any better than this, she thought.

Until the middle of the day when she suddenly realised that her period was late. She calculated mentally. Not just late—*a whole week late*, and she was never late.

For a moment she couldn't breathe. *What if she was pregnant?* And why, why, *why* hadn't she waited to go on the Pill and insisted on using condoms as well, before she'd made love with Jared?

She took a deep breath, knowing that she was being ridiculous. OK, so the only form of contraception that was one hundred per cent effective was total abstinence, but condoms still had a pretty good success rate. She and Jared had been really, really careful. And she was thirty years old, so her fertility level was lower than when she'd fallen pregnant last time. She only had one Fallopian tube working, making the chances of falling pregnant even lower. This was probably just a stupid glitch.

But how many other women had been caught

out that way? How many teenage girls had fallen pregnant after just one time? How many women, nearing menopause and thinking that their fertility was practically zero, had taken a risk and discovered they were having a 'happy accident'? She knew of several colleagues who hadn't planned their last babies.

And what if history repeated itself? What if she was pregnant and it was another ectopic pregnancy? What if, this time, she lost absolutely everything?

There was only one way to find out. And she was going to have to be brave and face it.

At lunchtime she went out and bought a pregnancy test kit. With every step back towards the hospital her legs felt as if they were turning into lead, heavy and dragging.

The last time she'd bought a pregnancy test she'd been so excited, so hopeful. She had actually run to the bathroom, because she'd so desperately wanted it to be positive—she'd wanted to know the result that very second.

This time, taking a pregnancy test felt more

like a sentence of doom. Something she had to nerve herself to do. Panic made her hands shake as she opened the box. It took her three goes to open the test kit itself.

Oh, God. Oh, God. Oh, God.

Please don't let her be pregnant.

Please don't let the nightmare happen all over again.

Please don't let that low, dragging pain start as a nag and then flare into agony.

Please don't let her lose her last chance.

Time felt as if it was wading through treacle as she washed her hands and kept an eye on the test stick. One line in the window to let her know that the test had worked.

She felt sick. The line in the next window would tell her yes or no.

'Please let it be no. Please let it be no. Please let it be no.' The words were ripped from her, low and guttural.

But she knew that begging wasn't going to change a thing. The test stick was measuring the level of a hormone in her urine: human chorionic gonadotropin, which was produced by the placenta after fertilisation.

Then again, a negative result could be just as bad because it might mean that the embryo hadn't implanted yet—or that it had implanted in the wrong place. Just as it had before.

She stared at the next window. One line formed, and then a second.

Positive.

Her knees went weak and she sat down heavily.

And then there was the window to tell her how many weeks since conception…

She stared at the window until the words finally penetrated her brain. *Three weeks plus.* She and Jared had first made love three weeks and two days ago. Now she thought about it, it had been smack in the middle of her cycle. The most fertile stage. Which would make her five weeks and two days pregnant now.

No, no, no, no, no.

Nearly three years ago, at this stage, that meant that in one week and one day's time…

Her stomach heaved, she dropped the test stick and was promptly sick in the sink.

Bailey washed her face afterwards while she tried to think about what to do.

She was going to have to tell Jared; but she had absolutely no idea what she was going to say. Or what was going to happen next. He'd said he wanted kids one day. But they hadn't been together that long. This was way too soon. She didn't think Jared was the kind of man who'd walk away, or who paid towards a child's upbringing but had no emotional involvement with the baby whatsoever—yet something else worried her. Would he want the baby more than he wanted *her*?

Panic really had turned her into a gibbering, raving idiot. She was always so together, so organised. Not knowing what to do next just wasn't in her make-up. And it freaked her out even more that she was reacting like this. That all her common sense had vanished into thin air. That she couldn't think rationally.

What the hell was she going to do?

Right now, her parents were in Italy. She knew that all she had to do was pick up the phone and her mother would get on the next plane to London to be with her but that wasn't fair; her parents deserved a chance to enjoy having a holiday around their wedding anniversary. Her brothers were up to their eyeballs running the restaurant, so it wouldn't be fair to talk to them about it, either.

Then there was Joni. But how could Bailey dump something like this on her best friend, when Joni should have the chance to enjoy her own pregnancy without any shadows?

Besides, Jared was the one she *really* needed to talk to.

Today was one of her clinic days, so she wouldn't see him during working hours. She knew she could call him—but she didn't trust herself to make any sense on the phone. She had a nasty feeling that she'd start crying as soon as she heard his voice. The last thing she wanted to do was to panic him by sobbing uncontrollably and mumbling incoherent fragments at him. This conversation needed to be face-to-face. Rational. Together.

But her brain was so fried that she couldn't even remember what they'd arranged to do this evening. Was she meeting him at his place? At hers? Somewhere else?

'For pity's sake, Bailey Randall, get a *grip*,' she told herself sharply.

But she couldn't. She felt as if she was scrabbling around in the dark, wearing oversized boxing gloves.

She grabbed her phone and texted Jared. Can you meet me at my place after work?

Jared looked at Bailey's message on the screen of his phone: Can you meet me at my place after work?

Odd. They'd planned to go out for a pizza after work and then to the cinema. He was meeting her at the Tube station. Had she forgotten? Or had something happened that meant they had to change their plans?

Sure. Is everything OK? he texted back.

OK, she replied.

That was very un-Bailey-like. She was normally much chattier than this. Or maybe she was having a rough day in clinic and she was up to her eyes in work. Being busy might explain her forgetting their plans.

He was busy that afternoon, too, and didn't think anything more of it until she answered the door to him. Then he saw that her face was pale—paler than he'd ever seen it before—and her eyes were puffy, as if she'd been crying. 'Bailey? What's happened?' he asked.

She backed away before he could put his arms round her. 'You'd better come in and sit down.'

And now he was really worried. This definitely wasn't normal for her. The woman he'd been dating was warm and tactile. She liked being hugged, and he really enjoyed the physical side of being close to her. The fact that she'd just backed away… What was happening?

He followed her into the kitchen and she indicated the chair opposite hers.

'Do you want a drink?' she asked.

'No. I want to know what's wrong,' he said, sitting down. And his worry increased exponentially when he reached across the table to hold her hand and she pulled away.

'I'm, um…' She dragged in a breath. 'Well, the only way I can tell you is straight out. I'm pregnant.'

Jared wasn't sure what he'd been expecting, but it sure as hell hadn't been this.

Pregnant?

'But—how?' He knew the question was stupid as soon as the words left his mouth. They'd had sex. Which meant the risk of pregnancy. He shook his head in exasperation at his own ridiculousness. 'I mean, we were careful.'

'I know.'

'How far along are you?'

'Just over three weeks, according to the test.' She dragged in a breath. 'Five weeks since the start of my LMP.'

'OK.' He blinked, trying to clear his head.

Bailey was pregnant.

With his baby.

He'd been here before—sort of. When Sasha had told him that she'd had a termination. Saying that she didn't know whether the baby was his or not. Saying that she didn't want a baby anyway. Saying that she didn't want to be married to him any more.

This wasn't the same thing. At all.

But it was a hell of a lot more complicated. The last time Bailey had been pregnant it had been ectopic. She'd gone through enormous physical pain—and she'd lost part of her fertility as well as the baby. And the fear of it happening again had led to the breakdown of her marriage.

Right now, she was clearly panicking, worrying that history was about to repeat itself. Would that panic make her consider having a termination even before the embryo had implanted—and would she make that decision without him?

He pushed the fears away. Bailey wasn't Sasha. And Bailey needed his full support. He had to put his own concerns and feelings aside and put her first. And he needed her to know that he'd be there. Given how she'd pushed Ed away, she was likely to do the same thing with him—he was learning that this was the way Bailey coped. She'd already begun pushing him away by not letting him hold her and comfort her when she was clearly so upset.

Well, Jared wasn't Ed, either. He wasn't going to let her push him away. The future might be tricky, but they had a lot more chance of surviving it if they faced it together.

He didn't think she'd listen to him right now—panic would've stopped up her ears. Which left him only one course of action. He stood up, walked round to her side of the table, scooped her out of her chair and sat down in her place. Once he'd settled her on his lap, he wrapped his arms tightly round her. Now she'd know for sure that he wasn't going to let her go.

She wriggled against him. 'Jared, what are you doing?'

'Showing you,' he said simply. 'That I'm here.

That we're in this together. That I'm not going to let you push me away.'

She looked utterly confused. 'But—'

'But nothing,' he cut in gently. 'Oh, and just so you know—Bailey Randall, I love you.'

CHAPTER THIRTEEN

HE LOVED HER?

Bailey couldn't quite take this in. 'But…we've hardly…'

'It's too soon. I know. We haven't been dating long, we've both got baggage and we should both be taking this a hell of a lot more slowly.' Jared shrugged. 'But there it is. I don't know when it happened or how. It just *is*. I love you, Bailey. You make everything sparkle. My world's a better place with you in it. I know the very second you walk onto the football pitch at work, even if my back's to you and I haven't heard you speak, because the world immediately feels brighter.'

It was the nicest thing anyone had ever said to her.

But still the worry gnawed at her. He'd told her he wanted children. And she'd just told him she was pregnant. Why else would he say that he loved her? 'Are you saying this because of the baby?' she asked.

'No. The baby doesn't change anything about the way I feel about you.' He blew out a breath. 'But I guess there's something I ought to tell you. It's the wrong time to tell you, but if I don't tell you now then you'll be hurt that I didn't tell you when you eventually find out, and… Oh, hell, you'll be hurt if I do tell you.' He rested his forehead against her hair. 'I don't know how to say this.'

'You and Sasha had a baby?' she guessed.

'Not exactly,' he said.

She frowned. 'I don't understand.'

'She was pregnant,' he explained, 'but she didn't know whether the baby was mine or someone else's, because she'd been sleeping with another man, too. Until she told me, I didn't have a clue that she'd been having an affair, much less anything else.'

Bailey was too shocked to say anything. So Jared had been here before. Been hurt. And she'd just brought back all the bad memories for him, too.

'She, um, had a termination,' Jared said quietly. 'When I thought she was going on a girly weekend with her mates.'

'She didn't tell you until afterwards?'

'She didn't tell me,' he corrected softly, 'until the bank statement came through and it turned out she'd accidentally used the wrong debit card to pay for it.'

'How do you mean, the wrong debit card?'

'Sasha didn't work,' Jared explained. 'I used to put money into her account every month, because I didn't want her to feel that she had to check with me or ask me for money before she went out to lunch with her mates or had her hair done. That might've been the way our grandparents did things, but I thought it was important she should feel that she had money of her own.'

So Jared had done what he'd thought was the right thing, and it had come back to bite him.

He sighed. 'When I saw the payment to a private medical clinic, I realised something was wrong.' He gave a wry smile. 'I know I'm a sports medicine doctor, but I was a bit hurt that she hadn't talked to me about whatever medical thing was worrying her. I could've reassured her and maybe helped her get the right treatment. When she came home that night I asked her about it, and that's when she told me about the affair.' He swallowed hard. 'And the reason she'd been to the clinic was because she'd had a termination. She'd got rid of the baby without telling anyone what she was doing—without telling anyone at all. Not me, and not the other guy whose baby it might have been.'

Clearly the double betrayal had cut him to the bone.

'Don't get me wrong,' he said. 'I believe there are circumstances where a termination is the right choice. But I do think you should at least talk over all the options with your partner before you make a decision as life-changing as that.'

'And it wasn't the decision you would've made?' Bailey asked.

He shook his head. 'As I said, even if the baby hadn't been mine, we could've worked it out. Or at least tried to work it out. But then she came out with all this other stuff and I realised that even if the baby had definitely been mine, she would've done exactly the same thing. She didn't want a baby at all. She didn't want the changes it would make to her body.'

'That's…I don't know what to say,' Bailey admitted. 'That was hard on you.'

'On both of us,' Jared said ruefully.

'It wasn't your fault she had an affair, Jared.'

'Maybe, maybe not. My work took me away a lot, and that wasn't fair on her.'

Sasha had taken the choice away from Jared. Did he think Bailey would do the same? Was that why he was telling her this? Or was he telling her that he definitely wanted the baby? She swallowed hard. 'You said in the park, that time, that you wanted kids.'

'I do.' He paused. 'But that's not the be-all and end-all of a relationship, Bailey. You're pregnant with my baby, but that's not why I want to be with you. I want to be with you for *you*.' He took a deep breath. 'And right now I'm guessing that you're in a flat spin, worrying that history's going to repeat itself. This must be your worst nightmare. Your biggest fear come true.'

Her breath hitched. 'Yes.'

His arms tightened round her. 'I know you've had one ectopic pregnancy, but it doesn't mean that this one's definitely going to be ectopic as well.'

Brave, she thought, but misguided. 'We both know the risks of having another ectopic are higher in subsequent pregnancies.'

'It's a *risk*, not a guarantee,' he said. 'Let's start this again. You've just told me that you're pregnant. I know you're scared. I think I am, too. It's a huge thing. But this is amazing, Bailey. Really *amazing*. We're going to be parents.'

'What if...?' Again, she couldn't breathe. Couldn't say the words that haunted her.

'If it's another ectopic pregnancy or you have a miscarriage? Then we'll deal with it if and when that happens,' he said. *'Together.'*

And then she realised that he wasn't going to let her push him away. Even if she tried. He wasn't going to repeat his mistakes, and he wasn't going to let her repeat hers, either.

The bleakness and fear ever since she'd taken the pregnancy test suddenly started to recede. Only a little bit, but it was a start. 'You reckon?'

'I reckon.' He didn't sound as if he had any doubts. 'And I'll be brave and lay it on the line. I want you, Bailey. Yes, I'd like us to have children together—whether they're our natural children, whether we need IVF to help us or whether we adopt. But the non-negotiable bit is you. I love you, Bailey, and I want to be with you.'

He meant it. She could see that in his eyes. He'd been honest with her, and she owed him that same honesty. 'I want to be with you, too,' she said. 'But I'm scared that I'm going to make the same mistakes again. My marriage collapsed because I pushed Ed away, and I know I hurt him. I feel bad about that.' She blew out a breath. 'I don't want to hurt you like that,

Jared. Especially as I know you've already been through a rough time.'

'Then maybe we both need to do something different this time,' he said softly. 'Maybe we need to take that leap and trust each other—and ourselves.'

She nodded. 'This is a start.'

He took a deep breath. 'If you decide that you can't go ahead with the baby, then I'll support you. I'll be right by your side.'

Even though a termination was clearly a hot button for him, he'd support her if that was what she wanted.

But that was only one option. What about the really scary one? 'And what if—what if I *do* want to go ahead?' she asked.

'Then I'll still be right by your side. Nothing changes.'

He'd be there for her. Whatever. Regardless. Because he loved her.

'I'm not going to wrap you up in cotton wool—even though part of me wants to—because I know it will drive you insane. So I'll be whatever you need me to be. Though, to be fair, I'm not a mind reader,' he added, 'so you'll have to tell me if I get it wrong, instead of expecting me to work it out for myself. Because I'm telling you now that I probably won't be able to work it out.'

Trust him.

Take the risk.

Could she?

She thought about it. When she'd told him about her ectopic pregnancy, he'd been brilliant. He hadn't pushed her, he hadn't told her what to feel—he'd just held her and listened. He'd backed her in front of Lyle Fincham; he'd even said that if she left the club, so would he. And he'd just opened his heart to her, been totally honest with her.

She knew he'd be by her side all the way through her pregnancy. Not smothering her, not making the decisions for her—but he'd be there to discuss things, to help her see a way forward through all the worries. Just as he was here for her now—holding her, letting her know that he was there, supporting her.

So, yes, she could take the risk.

But there was something else she needed to tell him. Something important.

'I love you, too,' she said softly. 'Even when you're being stubborn and awkward and I want to shake you.'

'I'm glad we cleared that up,' he said dryly.

'And here I am, insulting you again when I'm trying to tell you something really important.' She leaned forward to kiss him. 'I didn't date anyone after my divorce. I never wanted to be with anyone again. I didn't want to take the risk of loving and losing. But I noticed *you*. Even though you annoyed me the very first time I met you, at the same time I noticed your eyes were the colour of bluebells.'

'Bluebells...' He looked amused.

She cuffed him. 'Stop laughing at me. I'm trying to be romantic.'

'Are you, now?'

She loved that sarcastic Scottish drawl. 'And

then you trained with me.' She went hot at the memory and her breath caught. 'Your biceps,' she whispered.

He nuzzled her earlobe. 'Yeah. Your back. I hope you know you gave me some seriously hot dreams.'

Just as she'd dreamed about him. 'You danced with me at my best friend's wedding. You kissed me.'

'I wanted to do a lot more than dance with you. And kiss you. Except you got spooked.'

'I know. It scared me that I wanted you so much, Jared. I didn't want to be attracted to anyone. I didn't want to love anyone again. But then,' she said simply, 'there you were. And it happened. I fell for you. As you said, I don't know how or where or when. I just *did*.' She paused. 'I love you.'

'Good.'

She kissed him again. 'So what are we going to do about this?'

'Given that you're expecting my baby and we haven't had a proper courtship?' he asked. 'I guess we're just going to have to take each day as it comes. But one thing I promise you is that I'll always have your back,' he said. 'Just as I know you have mine—I haven't forgotten the way you stood up to Lyle Fincham on my behalf.'

'You stood up for me, too,' she pointed out. And then suddenly it was clear as the panic ebbed further and further away. 'You make me feel safe, Jared. And you make me feel as if I can do everything I'm too scared to do.'

'And you make me want to be a better man,' he said.

'You're already enough for me, just as you are,' she said.

He held her closer. 'So I'm going to ask you properly. I don't have a ring, but that's something we'd choose together later in any case.' He kissed her, then gently moved her off his lap and dropped to one knee in front of her. 'Bailey Randall, will you do me the honour of being my wife?'

'Yes. Absolutely yes,' she said, drawing him

to his feet and kissing him. 'I think I'd like a quiet wedding, though.' Particularly as it would be second time round for both of them. Their second chance.

'We can do whatever we want,' Jared said. 'Whether you want a tiny church or a deserted island or a remote castle—whatever you want, that's fine by me. I don't care where we get married or how, just as long as you marry me.'

'I'd like just our family and closest friends there—the people who mean most to us,' she said. 'And then maybe a meal afterwards.'

'Maybe a little dancing. I quite like the idea of dancing with my bride,' he mused. 'And a wedding cake made by Rob.'

'White chocolate and raspberry,' she suggested.

He grinned and kissed her. 'Good choice. I agree.'

'When did you have in mind?'

'I would say as soon as we can, which means a fortnight, but that might be rushing it a tad,' he said. 'So how about…say…six weeks from now?'

Around the time of the twelve-week scan. *If* the baby was even viable. If she wasn't in the middle of another ectopic pregnancy.

'What if it goes wrong?' she whispered.

Luckily he seemed to realise that she was talking about the baby and not them. 'It's not going to stop me loving you and wanting to be married to you,' he said.

'But what if everything goes wrong and I can't have children?' She dragged in a breath. 'You said you wanted children.'

'There are other ways,' he said. 'Adoption. Fostering. Or even if it's just the two of us and a dog and a cat, and we just get to spoil our nieces, nephews and godchildren. We'll still be a family. We'll be together.'

He really, really believed in them.

And the strength of that belief nearly made her cry.

'Agreed. Six weeks,' she said. 'On a weekend?'

'Or a weekday. Whenever they can fit us in.'

He paused. 'I need to buy you an engagement ring. Maybe we can go shopping at the weekend.'

She smiled. 'That's not important. It's not about the jewellery. It's about how we feel.'

'I know. But I still want to buy you an engagement ring.' He hammed up his accent. 'I'm traditional, you know.'

'And you're going to marry me in a kilt?'

That made him laugh. 'No.'

She rolled her eyes. 'Spoilsport.'

'It might clash with your dress. Anyway, we need a ring first. We're going to do this properly, Dr Randall.'

She laughed and kissed him. 'OK. An engagement ring it is.'

He paused. 'Though maybe you should meet my family before I give you the ring.'

'And we need to tell mine,' she said. 'Be warned, there will be a party. And nobody parties like Italians.'

'No? Try the Scots,' he said. 'Now, *we* can party all night.'

She smiled. 'So your family likes partying as much as mine? We might have a bit of trouble talking them into a quiet wedding.'

'No. They love us. They'll back us in having exactly what we want,' Jared said. 'My family's going to love you.'

'Mine already likes you.'

'Then we're going to be just fine.' He sat down on the chair again and pulled her back onto his lap. 'I love you, Bailey.'

'I love you, too.'

'And I know you're still scared—so am I,' he admitted. 'But we can talk to the experts and make sure we know what all our options are.'

'They did tell me last time,' she said, 'but I didn't really take any of it in. I guess I was a bit too shell-shocked.'

'Then we'll ask again,' he said. 'We'll get the first appointment we can and ask for an early scan—maybe even more than one, until we're sure this pregnancy definitely isn't ectopic—and the one thing I promise you is that your other tube isn't going to rupture. Because if it *is* another ectopic, we'll do something before that happens.'

She swallowed hard. 'Have a termination, you mean.'

He nodded. 'But it won't be because we don't want the baby. It'll be because the baby doesn't have a chance of survival and it's a risk to your health, which isn't the same thing at all. And I will be right by your side, holding your hand, all the way.'

Giving her courage when she faltered. And letting her give him courage in the bits he found difficult. A true partnership. The same team. That worked for her. 'That,' she said, 'is a deal.'

The next morning, Bailey booked an appointment with her GP. She texted Jared to let him know the time and where to meet her, just in case he could make it.

He made it. She was pretty sure he'd had to call in some favours to do it, but she was glad that he'd kept his promise to her: he was right by her side, all the way.

He held her hand while she told the GP about her previous pregnancy and the GP rang through to the hospital to book her in for an urgent scan.

And he was right by her side as they walked through the corridors towards the ultrasound department at the hospital later that afternoon.

'I'm scared,' she whispered.

'I know you are, but I've got a good feeling about this.' His fingers tightened round hers. 'And, whatever happens, I'm here and I'm not going away.'

No matter what she did or said, he wasn't going to let her push him away. He wouldn't let her repeat her mistakes. Funny how that made everything feel so much safer.

Jared held her hand while the trans-vaginal scan was done, and he didn't say a word about the fact that her fingers were so tightly wrapped round his that she must've been close to cutting off his circulation. He was just there. Solid. Immovable. Her personal rock.

'Dr Randall, I'm absolutely delighted to say,' the ultrasonographer said with a broad smile, 'that you have an embryo attached very firmly to the wall of your placenta.'

The picture on the screen was just a fuzzy blob to both of them; they couldn't really make anything out at all.

But it was their baby.

In her womb, not in her Fallopian tube.

And the nightmare that had happened last time definitely wasn't going to happen again. *It wasn't an ectopic pregnancy.*

Bailey felt the tears spilling out of her eyes as she looked over at Jared; and she could see that his eyes were shiny with tears, too. 'Are you crying?' she whispered. Her big, tough, dour Scotsman, in tears?

'Yes, and I'm not ashamed of it. We're seeing our own little miracle,' he whispered back. 'I'm so happy. I want to climb on top of the hospital roof and yell it out to the whole world.'

The picture that put in her head made her smile but then the panic came crashing back in to spoil it. 'Not yet. We don't say a word to anyone, not until twelve weeks,' she said. Just in case she lost the baby. There were still no guarantees that everything would be all right. But at least they'd passed the first hurdle.

CHAPTER FOURTEEN

JARED'S PREDICTION ABOUT his family turned out to be spot on. Bailey adored Jared's family—particularly when Aileen, Jared's sister, took her quietly to one side and confided in her. 'We've all been so worried about him.'

'After Sasha, you mean?'

Aileen nodded. 'But he's seemed a lot happier lately. Now I've met you, I can see exactly why. And I'm so pleased you're joining our family.'

'Me, too,' Bailey said, and hugged her impulsively.

And her family was just as ecstatic when Jared and Bailey dropped in to announce the news of their wedding. And they insisted on having a small party with cake and champagne—including Jared's family—when Jared bought Bailey a very pretty sapphire-and-diamond knot.

* * *

To Bailey's relief, Jared didn't wrap her in cotton wool. Instead, he insisted that her life should be pretty much as it always was—only just not quite so intense on the exercise front. But he did move into her place, and he insisted on bringing her breakfast in bed every morning.

Bailey couldn't ever remember being this happy before.

It was hard not to share the news about the baby with her mum and Joni, especially as Joni was blooming with her own pregnancy, but Bailey was completely superstitious about it. She wasn't going to do anything the same this time. She wasn't even going to start looking at baby clothes, or nursery furniture, or baby name books, until they'd reached the twenty-week mark.

But she was glad that Jared had suggested getting married in six weeks' time, because planning everything would keep them both occupied. He'd already booked the register office and asked his oldest brother to be his best man. Her family had immediately offered to sort out the wedding breakfast and the wedding cake—raspberry and white chocolate, as she'd suggested. So all she had to do was sort out her bridesmaid, the dresses, the invitations and the flowers.

On Monday evening, after the yoga class— and luckily Joni had told Bailey exactly which bits Jenna had suggested to tone down during pregnancy, so she was able to do the same without having to ask—she and Joni had their usual catch-up over a chicken salad.

'There was something I wanted to ask you, Joni,' she said. 'How do you fancy being a bridesmaid again?'

Joni stared at her in shock. 'You and Jared, you mean? But…you stopped talking about him. I thought it had gone wrong. And, um—well, I thought you'd tell me about the break-up when you were ready.'

Bailey grinned. 'In answer to your questions—yes, yes, yes, and we've sorted it out so there's nothing to talk about.'

'You and Jared,' Joni repeated.

'Me and Jared,' Bailey confirmed.

Joni hugged her. 'That's the best news ever.'

'Don't cry, or you'll start me off,' Bailey warned, seeing the telltale glitter in her best friend's eyes.

'Sorry. It's hormones making me so wet and crying over everything,' Joni said.

Me, too, Bailey thought, but hugged the secret to herself.

'So when is it all happening?'

'Um, that would be…a little under six weeks.'

Joni looked shell-shocked. 'That soon?'

Bailey shrugged. 'We couldn't see any reason to wait. The reception's going to be at the restaurant, Rob's doing the cake, the register office is booked…so all I need to do is sort out flowers, dresses, and ask you if Olly's band would come and play during the meal.'

'I'm sure they will—in fact, I'll ring him now.' A couple of minutes later she hung up. 'Deal. Olly says he needs to know what the "our song" is.'

'I have no idea.' Bailey spread her hands. 'I guess I'll have to ask my fiancé what he thinks.'

'And I'll go dress-shopping with you any time.'

'Good. That means this Saturday,' Bailey said.

And by the end of Saturday she had the perfect dress—a skater-style strapless dress in deep red velvet that wouldn't let her pregnancy show, even in another five weeks' time, with matching shoes. Joni had a similar dress in ivory with red shoes and a red sash, and her mother found a champagne-coloured suit.

'Look at us. We rock,' Bailey said, when they were dressed up and standing in front of the mirror.

'Jared's going to be totally bowled over. You look so beautiful,' Lucia said. 'You both do.'

They agreed on simple flowers—ivory roses for Bailey and red roses for Joni. The invitations were written and posted. And all they had to do then was hope for a sunny day.

Finally it was the Thursday of Bailey and Jared's wedding day. Bailey had spent the previous night at her parents' house, to preserve the tradition of not seeing the groom until the actual wedding. Jared had sent her a single red rose, first thing, with the message, 'I love you and I can't wait to marry you'—in his own handwriting, she noticed, rather than the florist's.

Joni and Aaron came over to help them get ready, and finally they were ready to go to the register office. As Bailey had been expecting, she and Jared were both interviewed by the registrar—in separate rooms so they wouldn't see each other until the wedding—and then finally the guests were all seated and it was time to walk into the room itself.

They'd arranged for Olly to play a song on acoustic guitar as she walked down the aisle on her father's arm—a love song from Jared's favourite rock band, with the mushiest words in the world, and she'd nearly cried the first time Jared had played it to her.

And her dour Scotsman—wearing morning dress rather than a kilt, but with a velvet bow tie to match her dress—lit up in smiles as he turned to watch her walk up the aisle.

'You look amazing,' he said. 'I love that dress. But, most of all, I love you.'

'I love you, too,' she whispered.

Every moment of the ceremony felt as if it had been engraved on her heart—from the registrar welcoming everyone to declaring all the legal wording.

'I do solemnly declare that I know not of any lawful impediment why I, Jared Lachlan Fraser, may not be joined in matrimony to Bailey Lucia Randall,' he said, and she echoed the declaration.

He took her hand. 'I call upon these persons here present to witness that I, Jared Lachlan Fraser, do take thee, Bailey Lucia Randall, to be my lawful wedded wife.'

And then, once they were legally married, the registrar smiled. 'You may kiss the bride,' she said, and Jared took Bailey into his arms, kissing her lingeringly to the applause of their family and friends.

Once the registration was complete and they'd checked the entry was correct before signing it, there was time to take photographs on the marble staircase. And then, outside the register office, everyone threw dried white rose petals over them.

She smiled at Jared. 'This is even better than snow,' she said.

'Especially as it won't result in broken bones on the football pitch,' he said.

She grinned. 'Indeed, Dr Fraser.'

'Absolutely, Dr Fraser.' His eyes were full of love.

He helped her into the wedding car. There were some last photographs, and then the chauffeur drove them off. It was only when Jared stopped kissing her that she realised they weren't heading in the right direction for her family's restaurant.

'Um, excuse me, please?' she said to the driver. 'I think we're going in the wrong direction.'

'No, we're fine, ma'am,' he said with a smile.

'But we're going the opposite way to the restaurant. Would you mind turning round, please?'

'Sorry, ma'am, I have my orders,' he said.

'Orders?' She frowned. What orders? 'Jared, do you know anything about this?'

He looked blank. 'We already made the arrangements. We're going to your family's restaurant—aren't we?'

She frowned. 'Can I borrow your phone?'

'Sure.'

She rang her mother. Lucia made some completely unsubtle noises that were clearly meant to be static and didn't sound remotely like it. 'Sorry. This mobile phone signal is breaking up,' she said, and hung up.

'I'll try Joni,' Bailey said, but her bridesmaid did exactly the same as the mother of the bride.

'Let me try my mother,' Jared said. Bailey handed the phone back to him, but the result was the same.

'This is obviously their idea of a surprise,' he

said. 'Whatever they've planned, they're all in it together.'

'I'm not very keen on surprises,' Bailey said.

'Me, neither, but right now I don't think there's anything we can do but go with it.' Jared smiled at her. 'Their hearts are in the right place.'

'I know,' she said ruefully. 'Sorry. It's hormones making me grumpy. I love you.'

He kissed her. 'I love you, too, Dr Fraser.'

Then she realised they'd pulled up outside the football club. 'What are we doing here?' she asked.

'I have no idea,' Jared said.

Bailey's father opened the door with a beaming smile. 'Dr and Dr Fraser, this way, if you please.' He helped Bailey out of the car.

There was a red carpet unrolled outside, and Jared and Bailey exchanged a glance; both of them had a glimmer of an idea now of what was happening.

They followed the red carpet into the room that the club used for functions. As soon as they walked in, there was a massive cheer from everyone in the room and a flurry of confetti in the air. The walls had been decorated with hearts, balloons and a huge banner saying 'Congratulations, Bailey and Jared'.

She could see everyone there—their families and friends, everyone from the football club, and all her colleagues at the sports medicine unit.

Archie and Darren came up to them. 'We know you wanted to keep it quiet—but we wanted to throw a party for you because you're both so special,' Darren said, and hugged them both.

Bailey had to blink back tears. 'Did you arrange all this, Darren?'

The boy nodded shyly.

'It was all his idea,' Archie said. 'He went to see Lyle about it, and Lyle got Mandy to help him with the details. He's been talking to both sets of parents and to your best friend, Bailey.'

'I don't know what to say,' Bailey said, 'except this is fantastic—thank you so much!'

The food was fabulous, and the centrepiece

was an amazing wedding cake made by her brother. No wonder he'd refused to let her see it, as it was a lot bigger than the one she'd planned—it was the same raspberry and white chocolate cake, but scaled up for many more guests.

'I can't believe you kept it all a secret,' she said to Rob. 'And that cake is just stunning.'

'Anything for my little sister,' he said, 'and the man who made her smile again.'

Finally it was time for the speeches. Jared stood up. 'This wasn't quite what we'd planned for the reception, so I don't have a huge speech. I'd just planned to thank my bride for making me the happiest man alive and I'm going to stick with my plan—well, almost.' He smiled. 'Some of you know that something quite special happened to me when I was seventeen. I thought when I scored the winning goal in the championship that it was the happiest moment of my life, but I was wrong—because today is even better than that. Today, the love of my life married me. So I'd like to make a toast to her. To Bailey.'

'To Bailey,' everyone echoed.

'And I'd also like to thank our family and friends, who managed to surprise us this afternoon as much as we surprised them with the announcement of our wedding,' he said. 'You're all fantastic and we love you.'

Jared's oldest brother gave a short, witty best-man's speech. And then it was the turn of the father of the bride; Paul was almost in tears. 'There's so much I could say—but I want to keep it short and sweet. Bailey's the apple of my eye, and I couldn't find a better son-in-law than Jared. So I want to wish Bailey and Jared a long, fabulous life together.'

Darren stood up next. 'I know I don't really have the right to do this, because I'm not family, but I wanted to make a tiny speech, too.'

'You organised our reception, so I think you earned the right,' Jared said with a smile. 'Go for it.'

Darren took a deep breath. 'I think most of

you know that I got into a bit of trouble a few months back, when I wasn't doing very well and I started drinking. Between them, Bailey and Jared straightened me out and gave me a second chance, and I owe them everything. Jared's been a brilliant father figure to me and I just wanted to say thank you. To Jared.'

A brilliant father figure. Yes, Bailey thought, he's going to be a brilliant dad. She squeezed her husband's hand under the table. He caught her eye and at her raised eyebrow he gave a small nod.

'In that case, I think I need to make a speech, too,' Bailey said, standing up. 'Doing this research into soft-tissue injuries at the football club has turned out to be the best decision I ever made, because it's how I met Jared. But what Darren just said really struck a chord with me. Jared's a brilliant father figure. And we've been keeping things under wraps a bit because—well, some of you know it's been a bit tricky for me in the past. But we'd like the world to know officially that Jared's going to be a dad in about six months' time.'

And the room erupted in a froth of cheering and champagne.

EPILOGUE

Six months later

JARED SAT ON the edge of the hospital bed, one arm round his wife and the other resting on the pink-swathed sleeping bundle in her arms.

'She has eyes the colour of bluebells—just like yours,' Bailey said dreamily.

'All babies have blue eyes,' Jared pointed out. 'She'll have brown eyes like you when she's older.'

'Not necessarily—my dad's eyes are blue,' she reminded him.

Jared stroked his daughter's cheek. 'She has your mouth.'

'And your nose.'

'She's beautiful. Our Ailsa.' He leaned over to kiss his new daughter. 'I thought on our wedding day I could never be happier than at that moment, but seeing her safely here in your arms and knowing you're both OK—life doesn't get any better than this.'

She smiled at him. 'Oh, I rather think it will. We have the first smile, the first word, the first step, the first "I love you, Daddy"—there's all that to come.'

'We're lucky. We got our second chance,' he said softly. 'And I love you, Bailey Fraser.'

'I love you, too,' she said. 'Always.'

* * * * *

MILLS & BOON®
Large Print Medical

September

BABY TWINS TO BIND THEM	Carol Marinelli
THE FIREFIGHTER TO HEAL HER HEART	Annie O'Neil
TORTURED BY HER TOUCH	Dianne Drake
IT HAPPENED IN VEGAS	Amy Ruttan
THE FAMILY SHE NEEDS	Sue MacKay
A FATHER FOR POPPY	Abigail Gordon

October

JUST ONE NIGHT?	Carol Marinelli
MEANT-TO-BE FAMILY	Marion Lennox
THE SOLDIER SHE COULD NEVER FORGET	Tina Beckett
THE DOCTOR'S REDEMPTION	Susan Carlisle
WANTED: PARENTS FOR A BABY!	Laura Iding
HIS PERFECT BRIDE?	Louisa Heaton

November

ALWAYS THE MIDWIFE	Alison Roberts
MIDWIFE'S BABY BUMP	Susanne Hampton
A KISS TO MELT HER HEART	Emily Forbes
TEMPTED BY HER ITALIAN SURGEON	Louisa George
DARING TO DATE HER EX	Annie Claydon
THE ONE MAN TO HEAL HER	Meredith Webber

MILLS & BOON®
Large Print Medical

December

MIDWIFE...TO MUM!	Sue MacKay
HIS BEST FRIEND'S BABY	Susan Carlisle
ITALIAN SURGEON TO THE STARS	Melanie Milburne
HER GREEK DOCTOR'S PROPOSAL	Robin Gianna
NEW YORK DOC TO BLUSHING BRIDE	Janice Lynn
STILL MARRIED TO HER EX!	Lucy Clark

January

UNLOCKING HER SURGEON'S HEART	Fiona Lowe
HER PLAYBOY'S SECRET	Tina Beckett
THE DOCTOR SHE LEFT BEHIND	Scarlet Wilson
TAMING HER NAVY DOC	Amy Ruttan
A PROMISE...TO A PROPOSAL?	Kate Hardy
HER FAMILY FOR KEEPS	Molly Evans

February

HOT DOC FROM HER PAST	Tina Beckett
SURGEONS, RIVALS...LOVERS	Amalie Berlin
BEST FRIEND TO PERFECT BRIDE	Jennifer Taylor
RESISTING HER REBEL DOC	Joanna Neil
A BABY TO BIND THEM	Susanne Hampton
DOCTOR...TO DUCHESS?	Annie O'Neil